Tyler lay ba[...]l shock. Zak [...]y of the big s[...] just very thoroughly kissed her.

Not the best move he had ever made in his life, Zak rebuked himself. First and foremost Tyler was a reporter—and reporters, in his experience, were after only one thing: a story.

Something he had just given her in spades!

Somehow, and he wasn't quite sure how, he was going to have to take a step backwards—no, several steps backwards. He groaned inwardly as he remembered the softness of Tyler's breasts beneath that little tee shirt. She had felt so good, her skin like velvet to the touch, her lips soft and responsive beneath his.

But of course she had been responsive, he acknowledged with self-disgust. Claiming that he had seduced her during this week's interview would be the icing on the cake as far as any female reporter was concerned!

THE PRINCE BROTHERS

Enter the glamorous world of these gorgeous men...

Enter the glamorous world of the movies when you read
about the love lives of the celebrity Prince brothers,
owners of the prestigious company PrinceMovies.

Each brother is super-successful in his field:

Arrogant, forceful and determined, the oldest, **Nik,**
is a movie director.
Enjoy his story in

PRINCE'S PASSION
October 2005

A former bad boy, **Zak** is now a world-famous actor,
known for being a charming rogue.
Meet him in

PRINCE'S PLEASURE
November 2005

And the youngest, **Rik,** is a screenwriter who's more
reserved than his brothers, but very charming.
You can read about his life in

PRINCE'S LOVE-CHILD
January 2006

PRINCE'S PLEASURE

BY
CAROLE MORTIMER

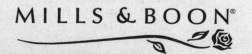

First published in Great Britain 2005
Harlequin Mills & Boon Limited,
Eton House, 18-24 Paradise Road, Richmond, Surrey TW9 1SR

© Carole Mortimer 2005

ISBN 0 263 84195 2

Set in Times Roman 10½ on 12 pt.
01-1105-46196

Printed and bound in Spain
by Litografía Rosés, S.A., Barcelona

CHAPTER ONE

'WHY was I under the impression you were a man?' Zak's mouth tightened as he stared at the woman standing outside his hotel suite.

Her brows rose over eyes so deep a brown they were like smooth melted chocolate. 'I have no idea, why were you?' she retorted.

He scowled, knowing exactly who was responsible for his erroneous impression. 'My brother Nik had something to do with it, I suspect!'

'Do I *look* like a man?' the woman teased.

In a word—no!

But, then, Zak hadn't known what she was going to look like, had he? He had simply been informed by Nik that he had agreed, on Zak's behalf, for a reporter named Tyler Wood to spend a week with him doing an exclusive interview. Nik, with his usual arrogance, had forgotten to mention that the reporter was young, beautiful, and female!

'Not in the least,' Zak allowed dryly, not knowing who he was angrier with, his brother, or this beautiful woman. 'Nik also forgot to mention that you're American.' He frowned, knowing he was going to find it much harder to keep a fellow countrywoman at a distance than he would have the typical English male hack he had been expecting.

Tyler Wood shrugged. 'Obviously your brother is a man of few words.'

Obviously.

And Zak hated being wrong-footed, damn it!

Despite the fact that Tyler Wood was dressed in green combat trousers, and a fitted black tee shirt, her short dark hair moussed into the spiky asexual style that was the fashion at the moment, there was no way she could be mistaken for anything other than female. Those mesmerizing long-lashed dark eyes apart, she had beautiful gamine features, with a small, snub nose and full, pouting lips, and her petite five foot two frame was definitely that of a woman, the trousers resting low on curvaceous hips, her breasts full—and obviously braless!—beneath the clinging material of her tee shirt.

'What's an American doing working for an English newspaper?' Zak was curious, knowing there were more than enough newspapers and journals in America to keep a reporter busy, without going to the trouble of crossing the Atlantic.

Tyler Wood stared at him for several minutes before answering rather casually, 'The same as an American actor in England, I suspect—working. Do you think I might come in?' she added pointedly.

Zak was aware that he couldn't keep her standing outside in the hotel corridor all morning, but he was still acclimatizing himself to the fact that the reporter who was to follow him around for a week was a gorgeous American woman.

He hadn't exactly been overjoyed when Nik had told him of the agreed interview, although he had accepted the reasons for it when his brother had explained to him that it had been done to protect Nik's new wife Jinx from the barrage of publicity that had been about to break over her unsuspecting head.

Tyler Wood had been the initial reporter to leak the

story, but after several conversations with Nik she had agreed to back off for a while in exchange for a week of interviewing Zak, an actor rarely out of the headlines, anyway.

But Zak had been expecting a man, and had thought the two of them could just spend a week together on the town. The reporter could then write up his interview, and everyone would go away happy. Discovering that Tyler Wood was a woman certainly put an end to that idea.

He drew in an impatient breath. 'I suppose you had better come in,' he allowed ungraciously as he opened the door wider for her to enter.

She reached to just under his chin, he discovered as she moved past him into the hotel suite, her almost elusive perfume that of some fresh-smelling flower.

She turned to smile bewitchingly at him, looking at him from under those ridiculously long, dark lashes.

Zak realized he was annoyed—annoyed because although he had always had a healthy relationship with the media, it had always been a relationship he had kept based on his own terms, and he had certainly never found one of their number attractive before. How the hell was he supposed to spend a week in this woman's company and keep her at arm's length at the same time?

She tilted her head to one side, looking at him speculatively now. 'I have to say, I always got the impression you were more—laid-back and charming than this...'

Zak was fully aware that that was the side of him he chose to present to the media. A side he was going to find increasingly difficult to present to Tyler Wood if he had to spend too much time in her company. Which, it appeared, he did...

He attempted to heal the slight breach he'd created. 'It's nine o'clock in the morning, I didn't get to bed until four o'clock; exactly how laid-back and charming do you want me to be?'

She gave a husky laugh. 'I'm sorry, Mr Prince. I didn't mean to imply that you were being less than gracious.'

Zak eyed her with suspicious blue eyes, knowing that, besides being less than charming, he looked less than his best, too. The party last night had been pretty wild, and he had probably drunk a little too much champagne too. He had literally only crawled out of bed five minutes before she had knocked on the door of his hotel suite.

Consequently he had quickly pulled on the black trousers and white silk shirt he had worn to go out the night before, running a hand briefly through the tousled blondness of his overlong hair, having no time at all to shave. Never one for exactly looking well dressed at the best of time, Zak still knew there was studied casualness and just plain scruffy—and he knew exactly which category he fitted into this morning!

'I am being less than gracious,' he apologized. 'Perhaps it's age? I used to be able to party all night and still be fresh and ready to work on the set by six o'clock the next morning. None of this is for the record,' he added quickly as she reached into one of the cavernous pockets in her trouser legs and brought out a notebook and pencil.

'Oh.' Those brown eyes darkened with disappointment before she placed the notebook back in the pocket to give him a considering look. 'Exactly how old are you?'

'Thirty-six. How old are you?' he came back.

'Twenty-six,' she answered without hesitation.

He nodded, having already guessed she was aged in her mid-twenties. 'And can you still party all night and then go to work in the morning?'

Once again she gave that husky laugh. 'I never could!'

Zak shrugged. 'Then perhaps there's hope for me yet.'

'Perhaps there is,' she agreed. 'Mr Prince—'

'Zak,' he corrected tersely. 'Mr Prince sounds like my brother Nik,' he explained.

And there could only ever be one Nik: arrogant, determined, forceful, a man totally confident of his own worth. Also now a happily married man, Zak acknowledged affectionately.

'I was just wondering, Mr—Zak,' she corrected huskily at his pointed look, 'if perhaps you feel you have been pressured into this interview by your brother and myself?'

'*Feel* as if I have?' he echoed incredulously. 'There's no *feel* about it, Miss—'

'Tyler,' she suggested with gentle mockery.

'Tyler.' He nodded impatiently. 'I was *pressured* into this interview by you and Nik. What's the interview for, anyway? Which publication?' he enlarged as she looked at him blankly. 'I'm pretty sure that the newspaper which carried your last article about Nik and Jinx isn't interested in this sort of exclusive interview.'

Was it his imagination, or did those huge brown eyes suddenly no longer quite meet his? Although he wouldn't be in the least surprised if she felt embarrassed about working for the newspaper that had plastered that story of Nik and Jinx all over its front page; a scandal-mongering tabloid was probably too kind a description of that particular rag!

Tyler gave him another one of those blindingly bright smiles. 'You're right, Mr Pr—Zak,' she corrected herself. 'But *The Daily Informer* does have a Sunday newspaper, with a glossy magazine supplement.'

'And you intend this interview to be published in that supplement?'

She turned to look out of the window at the London skyline. 'This is rather a magnificent view, isn't it?'

'Magnificent,' Zak agreed dryly. 'Tyler, I have the distinct feeling that you—' He broke off as the second knock of the morning sounded on his suite door.

'That will be my photographer,' Tyler Wood turned to reassure him as he scowled in the direction of the door.

'No,' Zak said firmly.

'Oh, but I think it might be,' she said, after glancing at the heavy watch that adorned the slenderness of her left wrist. 'I asked Perry to meet me here at nine-fifteen—'

'I wasn't disagreeing with your guess as to who might be on the other side of that door,' Zak elaborated. 'Merely stating that your agreement with my brother didn't include having a photographer trailing around with me for a week and shoving a camera into my face every minute of the day.' At least, it had damn well better not have included one!

Those deep brown eyes widened protestingly. 'But I'll need photographs to go with the article—'

'And you can have them,' he said. 'At the end of the week. At my convenience.'

Tyler looked as if she would like to argue that particular condition, but one look at his face must have convinced her she would be wasting her time. 'Okay,' she agreed. 'I'll just go and tell Perry, and then we can continue—'

'I'm actually going back to bed, Tyler,' Zak cut in, 'but if you would like to, I have no objection to you joining me there so that we can "continue"...?' He eyed her challengingly, still far from happy at having been pressured into this situation in the first place, and even less happy about it now that he had met the woman who was to be his shadow for a week.

If it weren't for the fact that he loved and respected his older brother, and if he didn't think so highly of Nik's wife, then Zak would have quite simply told Tyler what she could do with this 'exclusive interview'!

In fact, it might still come to that!

Tyler looked at him narrowly. 'I have a feeling you're enjoying playing with me, Zak,' she said finally.

'Under other circumstances, I'm sure that I would,' he taunted, rewarded by the sudden flush to her cheeks. 'But today? Right now? With a photographer standing on the other side of the door?' He shook his head. 'All I want at this moment is to go back to bed. Alone,' he added with finality.

'Of course,' she agreed lightly, walking over to the door with long, determined strides. 'Perhaps we can meet up again later this afternoon? Without the photographer.'

'Perhaps we can,' Zak conceded. 'Be sure to telephone first, though, hmm?' he added mockingly. 'I would hate to shock your delicate sensibilities by having you find me here with someone.' He raised dark blond brows.

Tyler Wood paused with her hand on the door handle. 'My sensibilities really aren't all that delicate, Zak. In fact, it was a pleasant surprise to find you here alone this morning.'

'Touché.' Zak nodded an appreciative acknowledgement of her sharp comeback.

She paused before opening the door. 'Tell me, when you worked with John Devaro last year—'

'Not another John Devaro fan!' he groaned before answering her. 'Yes, he really is as good-looking as he appears on screen. Yes, he really is a very funny guy. Yes—'

'I was actually only going to ask you if you felt in the least threatened by the fact that his name appeared above yours on the credits,' Tyler interrupted dryly.

Zak was taken aback at the unexpectedness of the attack—for attack it certainly was. 'The two of us talked it over and decided we would go alphabetically.'

'Oh.' She nodded. 'See you later, then!' A slight smile curved her lips as she let herself out of the hotel suite.

Perhaps there was more to Tyler Wood, after all, than a pair of melting chocolate-brown eyes and a stunning smile? Maybe he had underestimated the fact that she was a woman, an American one at that, trying to make it in a country that wasn't her own, in a profession that was often dominated by men.

And what if he had underestimated her? As he saw it, he had two choices where she was concerned.

Considering the way she seemed to get his hackles up without even trying, he could carry on being this obnoxious and uncooperative, or he could give in to the attraction he felt towards her and try charming her into his bed. He was damned if he didn't, and damned if he did!

Not much of a choice, really.

CHAPTER TWO

'ARROGANT bastard!' Perry scowled as the two of them made their way across the large hotel reception area to the huge revolving door that led out onto the street.

Tyler couldn't exactly blame him for being disgruntled at Zak's decision not to have a photographer following him around all week; the two of them had worked together on and off for six months now, and nothing like this had ever happened to them before.

Posing the question, had Zak realized there was more to this interview than at first appeared?

'Don't worry about it,' she assured Perry as they stepped out into the warming sunshine. 'I'm sure you'll be able to manage without his cooperation; you always have in the past.'

'And I'm sure I will this time,' Perry acknowledged with satisfaction. 'Although I would much rather have spent the time openly with the two of you rather than creeping around in the background.'

Tyler was well aware that for most of the last six months Perry had wanted to make their relationship into something more intimate, which she had so far resisted.

It wasn't that she didn't like Perry, and he was certainly a good-looking guy with his overlong dark hair and warm blue eyes, she just didn't feel that way about him and considered him more like a brother than anything else. Much to his chagrin.

But she couldn't in all honesty become involved with someone, especially a friend like Perry, without telling him everything about herself—and that she had no intention of doing. No one was to know who or what she was; as far as anyone in England was concerned she was just Tyler Wood, rookie reporter, and that was the way she wanted it to stay.

'Although I should watch yourself with Zak Prince this week, if I were you,' Perry added teasingly. 'From what I've heard the man can't be alone with a woman for five minutes without trying to seduce her into his bed!'

Tyler grimaced. 'Going on his mood this morning, I don't think he can succeed too often!'

She knew that wasn't true, though... Of the three Prince brothers Zak was the good-natured charmer. The oldest, Nik, had remained arrogantly aloof from involvement until his recent marriage. The younger brother, Rik, was the more reserved of the three, keeping himself to himself most of the time.

But obviously nine o'clock on a Monday morning, after what had obviously been a full weekend, was a time when Zak was all out of charm!

It had been Nik Prince, before disappearing on his honeymoon yesterday, who had been the one to set up this morning's meeting for nine o'clock...

Had it been deliberate? That would have been a little unkind on Nik's part—to both Tyler and Zak. But, then, kindness wasn't an emotion very often attributed to the legendary Nik Prince!

He *had* done it on purpose, Tyler realized with dismay. It wasn't an auspicious beginning to a week spent in Zak Prince's company.

*   *   *

'Tell me,' she asked later that evening once she had finally managed to meet up with Zak Prince again in the hotel lounge; he had still been sleeping when she had rung him at four o'clock. 'I know what I'd done to anger your brother enough to arrange such an early meeting that it was guaranteed to annoy you, but what did you do?' She quirked dark brows over mischievous brown eyes.

'Very astute of you, Tyler.' Zak Prince smiled, much more relaxed this evening as he lounged back in one of the capacious armchairs, wearing ragged denims and a loose black tee shirt. 'With Nik—' he shrugged '—who knows? Although I actually think it was his idea of a joke.'

'Ha ha.' Tyler grimaced.

'Yeah.' Zak grinned.

Tyler could see exactly why this man had won three Oscars. His smile was charismatic, almost mesmerizing when taken into account with the rest of his looks: overlong hair the colour of ripe corn, eyes the blue of a perfect summer sky, his features rugged, as if hewn from stone.

Whoa! Tyler brought herself up short. She was here to find a new angle on Zak Prince for her story, not fall under his spell herself.

Because she was sure there was more to this man than the charismatic charmer he was usually portrayed as. There had been rumours, of course, of involvements with married women, and even the possibility that the success of the Prince brothers' movie company owed much to connections with the shady underworld—which was patently absurd! But there were always rumours about anyone successful; Tyler wanted to get to the truth.

'Anyway—' she straightened briskly '—I apologize for any misunderstanding this morning and I suggest we move on.'

'Move on to where exactly?' he teased.

Tyler frowned, knowing she hadn't quite phrased that correctly somehow. 'Background stuff this evening, I thought,' she ploughed on. 'Where you were born, family, what you're working on at the moment, things like that.'

'Look, Tyler, I don't want to tell you how to do your job—'

'But you're going to anyway?' she guessed.

He shrugged broad shoulders, seeming completely impervious to the female attention his presence was engendering. Most of the other women in the lounge were unable to take their eyes off him, not quite with their tongues hanging out, but pretty close, Tyler noted disparagingly.

'Most people already know the background stuff,' he dismissed, pausing to smile up at the waitress as she brought over the two mineral waters they had ordered.

He was right, of course; the three Prince brothers and their younger sister were the children of the legendary Damien Prince, an actor who had held the public in thrall for over thirty years, before his premature death over twenty years ago.

During the brothers' youth, Zak had always been the bad boy of the family, in and out of trouble during most of his teens, dropping out of school to take up acting like his father, and then finally finding his niche and settling down to being the charming rogue that he was now known for worldwide.

But all three Prince brothers, the principals in the

movie company PrinceMovies, were as successful in their own individual fields, Nik as movie director, Rik as screenwriter.

'You're right.' Tyler nodded, accepting that he was just stating a fact rather than being arrogant. 'I can probably look all that up.' She settled back in her armchair. 'So what do you have planned for this week?'

'Planned?' He took a sip of his mineral water.

She had seen Zak being interviewed, had watched several recordings of him on one of the leading chat shows. She knew that he wasn't usually this much hard work, that he normally responded easily and smoothly to questions put to him, his charm always in evidence.

But it wasn't this evening—again.

Did he know something? Did he suspect that this interview wasn't quite as straightforward as she wanted it to appear?

'The reason why you're here in England.' She smiled, determined not to let him know she was bothered by his lack of cooperation. 'After all, you're usually based in the States, so—'

'My older brother was married at the weekend, Tyler; isn't that reason enough for me to be here?'

She felt embarrassed colour warm her cheeks. 'Of course,' she acknowledged evenly. 'I just wondered at the reason for your *still* being here.'

'You did?' he murmured incredulously.

She shrugged. 'I doubt anticipation of this interview was enough to keep you here!'

'You doubt correctly,' he said. 'The première of *Gunslinger* is showing on Saturday; I think I'm expected to be there!'

She had done it again, Tyler recognized with an

inner groan. Of course the English première of Zak's most recent movie was taking place this coming Saturday. She had known that. She had just forgotten it.

Because she was too anxious to get to the real story? Probably. Well, she wouldn't make that mistake again. She needed an exclusive—something new to the market, a different angle, a story no one had written before. And she was convinced that this interview with Zak could give her the exclusive she was after.

'I'm sorry, Zak,' she apologized. 'I—'

'Tyler—' he sat forward in his chair, his expression almost pitying '—might I suggest, in an effort not to waste any more of my time, that you go away and do a little more research before we continue with this?'

She deserved the rebuke, she knew she did, but that didn't alter the fact that he didn't need to have made it. The legendary Prince charm! Huh, so far she had seen little evidence of it!

Which only convinced her all the more that this man was hiding something, that there was more of a story behind Zak Prince than anyone had ever discovered. But she *would* discover it!

She straightened. 'That won't be necessary, Mr Prince,' she told him tartly. 'I'm aware of the première at the weekend, I was simply enquiring as to whether or not you are working on something else in England at the moment?' She met his mocking gaze unblinkingly.

She had guts, he would give her that. Guts, and a little anger too at the moment, if that glint in those chocolate-brown eyes was anything to go by.

Not surprising, really. He wasn't exactly giving her

an easy time of it this evening. But then it wasn't in his job description to make life easy for reporters. The fact that he normally did didn't mean that he had to do so in the case of Tyler Wood.

He had no idea why she should be so different, and yet something about her made his hackles rise, his normally relaxed approach to the media deteriorating to this barbed exchange of barely concealed animosity.

He shrugged. 'I'm meeting with a director for lunch tomorrow to discuss the start of filming next week—no, you cannot be present at the meeting,' he added as he saw her eyes light up in anticipation.

A light that instantly went out as her gaze narrowed angrily. 'My agreement with your brother was that I would be allowed complete access to you for a week—' She broke off as he raised a sardonic eyebrow. 'Not *that* sort of access, Mr Prince,' she snapped.

'I usually make my own choices when it comes to *that* sort of access,' he gibed. 'And your agreement was with my brother, not me.' His voice had hardened. 'So there will be no inclusion in my meeting tomorrow.'

She opened her mouth as if to argue the point, and then closed it again to stare across at him in total frustration.

Zak gave her a considering look. 'Tell me again what sort of magazine this interview is for, Miss Wood?'

'The usual sort of Sunday supplement,' she answered abruptly.

Was it his imagination, or had those brown eyes become slightly guarded again? 'The "usual" sort,' he repeated softly, once again having the feeling that

Tyler Wood was acting evasively. And she wasn't very good at it.

Her chin rose challengingly. 'I thought *I* was the one conducting the interview, Zak, not the other way round!'

'I'm just curious to know a little more about the woman I'm expected to take around with me all week. After all,' he added as she would have spoken, 'most people are going to assume that you're the latest woman in my life.'

'The latest in a *very* long—' She grimaced her dismay as she realized what she had just said. 'I shouldn't have said that. It's just that—'

'It's the truth…?' he jeered.

'No! I mean—well, yes, it is the truth. But I still shouldn't have said it.'

'No, you shouldn't,' Zak acknowledged dryly. 'But it's probably the most honest thing you've said all evening!'

Her eyes widened. 'I beg your pardon?'

'Granted.'

Her mouth firmed. 'I have no idea what you're talking about, Mr Prince. Are you implying I've been dishonest with you?'

Were her hands trembling slightly? He couldn't be sure as she hastily clasped those hands together. 'You aren't the only one with connections, Tyler,' he added, sure now that she had definitely gone paler. 'And this afternoon I made a few phone calls in order to check up on you.'

The colour did drain completely from her cheeks now. 'Oh, yes?' she said airily. 'And what did you learn?'

Zak looked at her with narrowed eyes, more convinced than ever that she was hiding something. 'Not a lot, as it happens. The press, it seems, can be pretty close-mouthed when it comes to one of their own. However, I did learn that you're considered a good reporter, if a little inclined to get too emotionally involved.' He paused before making his next statement. 'Also, that you had a blazing row with your editor a couple of weeks ago, which apparently culminated with him threatening to fire you…'

Her eyes were huge brown pools of melted chocolate as she met his gaze unflinchingly. 'Well, he doesn't seem to have carried out that threat, does he? Because I'm still employed,' she retorted.

'Apparently not,' he conceded, his mouth tightening. 'Out of interest, what did the two of you argue about?'

Tyler shook her head. 'I really don't think that is any of your business.'

He shrugged. 'I just wondered if it might have had anything to do with the little agreement you came to with my brother?'

'Of course not,' she snapped. 'Now if we could stop talking about me and concentrate on you…?' she said pointedly.

He sat forward. 'I'll keep asking until I find out the truth about you, Tyler,' he warned.

Tyler closed her notebook with a decisive snap before secreting it away in one of those many pockets on her combat trousers. 'Until today, I really believed all the things written and said about you in the media: that you're charming, not in the least difficult to work with, affable even!' She gave a disbelieving snort of derision. 'When in fact you're really exceptionally rude, extremely difficult to work with, and not even the tiniest bit affable!'

Zak reached across the tabletop and easily clasped her arm as she would have stood up, his fingers like steel bands. 'Is that what you intend writing in your article?' Despite the fact that he had set out to be as unpleasant as possible, he wasn't used to people disliking him, and found that he didn't particularly like the experience.

He also discovered that he liked the feel of Tyler's skin against his fingers. It was soft and silky to the touch, making him wonder if the rest of her body felt as sensuous and warm.

'Relax, Tyler,' he told her gently. 'We haven't finished talking yet.'

She looked across at him coolly. 'Do you want me to hang around just so that you can insult me some more?'

His mouth twisted into a smile. 'I'm all out of insults at the moment—but if you give me a few minutes...! Besides, we're drawing attention to ourselves.' He looked pointedly around the lounge to where quite a lot of people, several men included now, were openly staring at them.

'You're the one drawing attention to us,' she corrected him tautly, at the same time sitting back abruptly, releasing her arm from his grasp as she did so.

Zak watched as she ran the fingers of her other hand over the spot where he had held her. Both of her hands were completely bare of rings, and were long and slender, with delicately tapered fingers. He found himself wondering what it would feel like to have those fingers moving caressingly over his bare chest and back. And other parts of his body...

'We were discussing the argument you had with your editor,' he reminded her, angry with himself for having those thoughts about Tyler; she was a reporter, for goodness' sake!

She shook her head, her spiky hair gleaming almost auburn in the overhead lighting. '*You* may have been, I don't believe *I* was.' She met his gaze boldly over the rim of her glass as she took a sip of the mineral water.

Zak suppressed his feelings of irritation with difficulty, finding that this woman pressed buttons in him that he normally kept well away from the public eye— and he didn't mean physical ones! Although God knew she was attractive enough...

'What shall we talk about, then?' he mocked. 'The fact that you and the handsome photographer Perry Morgan are apparently inseparable? Or shall we—? Going somewhere, Tyler?' he asked as she put her glass down on the table with obvious force before moving to stand up.

Except she didn't quite make it, all the colour draining from her face before she collapsed back into the chair, her eyes closed, her breathing shallow.

'What the hell?' Zak had been propelled forward as she fell, moving down on his haunches beside her chair now. 'Tyler!' He shook her shoulder slightly. 'Tyler, speak to me, damn it!' he ground out forcefully.

She seemed to find the strength to open one eye and glare at him. 'Go away,' she muttered weakly.

He ignored that, and straightened before bending down and easily sweeping her up into his arms.

She weighed next to nothing, he discovered as he began to stride purposefully across the lounge with her still in his arms, totally immune to the avid stares the two of them were receiving, his expression one of grim determination.

'What do you think you're doing?' Tyler gasped, both eyes open now as she began to struggle in his arms.

'I would have thought that was obvious!' Zak didn't even glance down at her as he stepped into the waiting lift.

'It is, but—where are you taking me?' She was struggling even harder to sit up in his arms.

'My hotel suite,' he informed her. 'And stop struggling like that; you'll only end up hurting yourself,' he said as his arms tightened about her. He had no idea what was wrong with her yet, and until he did she wasn't going anywhere!

'You're definitely making an exhibition of us now,' Tyler protested as the two people waiting to get into the lift stared at them in shocked surprise as Zak stepped out with her still cradled in his arms.

'Do I look as if I care?' he dismissed impatiently as he used the key-card to get into his hotel suite, kicking the door shut behind him to stride over to the sofa and lay her down on it. 'Don't move,' he instructed her before moving over to the mini-bar, all the time keeping one eye on her as he searched through the array of alcoholic drinks there.

Although she didn't seem to be making too much of an effort to get up now, once again lying back with her eyes closed, her cheeks still deathly pale.

Either she really was ill, or this was some sort of elaborate ploy on her part to keep this interview alive.

It certainly wouldn't be the first time a woman had tried something like this on him in order to get into his hotel room, although, he had to admit, it wasn't usually with an interview in mind!

But if it should turn out that was what Tyler Wood was doing, then she was going to find out exactly how 'exceptionally rude' he could be!

CHAPTER THREE

'WHAT are you doing!' Tyler gasped, eyes wide as Zak raised her head and tipped some liquid into her mouth. Fiery liquid that burned as it went down her throat. 'No!' she protested, desperately trying to push his hand away, and not succeeding as he forced another mouthful of the foul-tasting liquid down her throat. 'What was that?' she groaned as he placed her head back on the sofa.

'Brandy,' he told her with satisfaction. 'Guaranteed to—'

'Make me ill,' she finished heavily. 'Even more so on an empty stomach.' A very empty stomach. In fact, it was because she hadn't eaten anything, since a hurried slice of toast for breakfast this morning, that she had collapsed in the first place.

She had been dismayed when she had first moved to London at how high the cost of living was here, her reporting job not exactly earning her big bucks. So, in order to survive on those wages, as she had sworn she would when she'd walked out of her sumptuous home in New York with claims to her family that she could make it on her own, she had had to economize on things. Like eating.

Bread, milk and cereals were cheap, as well as being quite nourishing, which was just as well, because it was what Tyler had mainly been living on for the last six months, with the odd hamburger thrown in here and there as a treat.

'Why do you have an empty stomach?' Zak probed, shrewdly attacking the relevant part of her statement. 'It's nine o'clock at night, so why haven't you eaten dinner yet?'

Because dinner was a luxury she could rarely afford. Lunch, either, for that matter. Although having eaten either wouldn't have lessened the effect the brandy was going to have on her any second now.

'I have an allergy.' She ignored his questions, trying to sit up. 'And if you don't get me to the bathroom in the next ten seconds I'm going to be ill all over this expensive carpet!'

'An allergy?' Zak Prince repeated with a dark scowl, making no effort to step forward and help her. 'What sort of allergy—damn it, Tyler...!' he rasped in disbelief as she put her head over the side of the sofa and was indeed ill all over the carpet.

As predicted.

It had been the surprise of her life to discover, on entering college, and the round of parties that had followed, that alcohol of any kind caused this reaction in her.

'What—how—what sort of allergy?' Zak Prince queried as he came back from the bathroom with a couple of towels, handing one to Tyler and throwing the other one over the mess on the carpet.

'To alcohol,' she had time to answer him before she was ill once again.

Not that this could last for too long; there was really nothing in her stomach for her to be ill with except that slice of toast and liquid!

Although it was unpleasant enough while it lasted, Tyler acknowledged half an hour later, equally exhausted and devastated that she had been sick in front of Zak Prince of all people. The fact that he was the one responsible for giving her the alcohol in the first place didn't lessen that feeling in the slightest!

'Damn it, you only had a couple of sips of the stuff!' he protested as he helped her to the bathroom to wash her face and clean her teeth, before easing her back onto the sofa.

'The amount doesn't seem to matter,' she explained. She was already feeling the start of the headache that usually followed one of these bouts. Not that there were any now that she simply avoided drinking alcohol.

Unless it was literally forced down her throat!

Sleep was the best thing for her now, although there wasn't too much chance of that until she had got herself back to her apartment...

It was dark when she woke up. Very dark. And very silent. Apart from the sound of steady breathing.

Tyler held her breath.

The sound of breathing continued.

Where was she?

More to the point, who was that breathing beside her?

She sat up with a start, groaning as she felt the pounding pain in her head.

'Are you okay?'

There was a movement beside her, and Tyler quickly closed her eyes as a light was switched on, its brightness only increasing the pounding in her head. As did the easy recognition of that voice!

'Tyler?' Zak repeated with concern.

What was she doing lying in bed beside Zak Prince?

How had she got here? More to the point, what was she still doing here?

The last thing she remembered was being violently ill, knowing she had to sleep, and then—nothing.

'Tyler, open your eyes and talk to me,' Zak Prince instructed forcefully, at the same time grasping her arms and shaking her slightly.

'If you don't stop doing that my head is going to fall off!' She gently lowered herself back onto the pillow.

Zak instantly stopped shaking her. 'Sounds like you have a hangover to me.' He sounded amused. 'Are you sure you hadn't been drinking before you met me last night?'

Her eyes shot open as she ignored the pain in her head to glare at him indignantly. 'I told you, I'm allergic to alcohol! One mouthful and I'm violently ill.'

'You sure are!' He grinned, leaning on his elbow to look down at her. 'In fact, I've never seen anyone as ill as you were last night. Before you blacked out, of course,' he added.

'I fell asleep,' she defended, and then winced at the loudness of her own voice. 'I fell asleep,' she repeated huskily, suddenly very aware of where they were, and of how close Zak Prince actually was. 'What time is it?' She turned her head slightly, having trouble trying to focus on the luminous clock on the bedside table.

The bedside table! She really was lying in bed with Zak. Both of them were fully dressed, she was relieved to see, but it was still a huge double bed the two of them lay in.

Zak peered past her at the clock. 'A few minutes after eleven o'clock,' he supplied.

'Oh, that's not so bad!' She sighed her relief. 'I've only been asleep for an hour or so—'

'A few minutes after eleven o'clock in the *morning*,' Zak enlightened her with a teasing smile.

'It can't be!' she protested, half struggling to sit up, and then falling back down again as she realized how close she was to Zak. 'If it's morning, then why is it still so dark?'

He shrugged broad shoulders. 'I always stay in this particular suite when I'm in London. If I'm working I never know when I'm going to get to bed and the curtains in here are so thick they cut out all the daylight.'

Tyler stared up at him now, her mouth open, her eyes wide with shock. Eleven o'clock in the morning! Did that mean she had been here all night?

Zak chuckled softly. 'Well, this isn't the usual reaction I get from a woman after we've spent a night in bed together!'

Tyler felt her face pale even more, her lips feeling slightly numb too. 'We—we haven't spent a night in bed together,' she finally managed to stutter.

'No?' He looked pointedly at their surroundings.

There was no denying that they were in a bedroom, nor that the two of them shared the same bed, but they certainly hadn't—they hadn't—had they…?

Her eyes were wide with anxiety as she looked up into Zak's face for some sign of exactly what had happened here last night, but his expression was unreadable as he looked at her beneath mockingly raised brows.

'You know, Tyler—' Zak reached up and pushed the short hair back from her brow, his fingers leaving a trail of fire where they touched '—I actually consider it extremely insulting that you could imagine I might take advantage of a woman who had just been violently ill all over my hotel suite!' His blue eyes looked as hard and gleaming as sapphires.

It did sound a little insulting, Tyler realized. In fact, a lot insulting. Although, considering his much-publicized reputation with women— No, she had better not even go there. Not if the now-dangerous glint in his eyes was anything to go by!

'Although the same certainly can't be said about twelve hours later!' he rasped just before his head swooped down and his lips claimed hers.

Tyler melted. Just melted. Her lips softened and clung to his, and her body responded avidly as he half lay across her, her hands moving up to thread her fingers in the silky softness of his corn-coloured hair.

Zak's mouth gentled, sipping, tasting, tenderly biting, causing first her lips to tingle, before the sensation spread to the rest of her body.

Then she felt as if she had been engulfed in flames as he suddenly deepened the kiss, her mouth opening wider to allow the hot, passionate intrusion of his tongue.

Her breasts, the nipples firm and inviting, pressed against the muscled hardness of his chest, a chest she longed to touch. Her hands thrust eagerly under his tee shirt, first stroking then lightly dragging her nails down—

'Housekeeping!' A sharp rap on the door accompanied the bright announcement.

Zak, whose fingers had just started to caress Tyler's generous, unfettered breasts beneath her top, shot away from her as if he had been stung. 'Damn, damn, damn!' he muttered. 'I forgot to put the ''Do Not

Disturb'' notice on the door last night before we went to bed!' He was scowling darkly as he swung his long legs off the bed and got up to walk over to the door.

Tyler lay back on the bed in total shock. Zak Prince, the golden boy of the big screen, had just very thoroughly kissed her. She had always wondered what was meant by that phrase, and now she knew. She had just been so 'thoroughly' kissed she still tingled all over and her legs felt shaky!

Not the best move he had ever made in his life, Zak rebuked himself even as he dealt with the cleaning lady standing out in the hallway. First and foremost, Tyler was a reporter, and reporters, in his experience, were after only one thing: a story.

Something he had just given her in spades!

Somehow, and he wasn't quite sure how, he was going to have to take a step backwards—no, several steps backwards. He groaned inwardly as he remembered the softness of Tyler's breasts beneath that little tee shirt. She had felt so good, her skin like velvet to the touch, her lips soft and responsive beneath his.

But of course she had been responsive, he acknowledged with self-disgust. Claiming that he had seduced her during this week's interview would be the icing on the cake as far as any female reporter was concerned!

'If you're hoping for a repeat performance I'm afraid you're going to be disappointed!' he gritted out as he turned from closing the door and found Tyler still luxuriating in the bed. 'I have that lunch appointment I told you about in—just over an hour,' he announced after glancing at his watch. 'But maybe we

can pick this up again later?' he added with a deliberately insulting raise of an eyebrow.

The colour flooded Tyler's cheeks as she scrambled
to sit up, turning away from him as she did so. 'Where
are my shoes?' she asked as she looked around
dazedly.

'Your *boots* are in the other room,' Zak said. He
still remembered his amazement the night before,
when he had gone to remove her footwear before putting her into bed and found she'd been wearing a pair
of yellow desert boots. 'Tell me, Tyler, do you wear
military clothes to make up for your lack of height
and stature?'

She stood up abruptly and frowned. 'And do you
take lessons in rudeness along with acting, or does it
just come naturally?'

'I've never really thought about it.' Rudeness
wasn't usually a part of his character; only Tyler
Wood, it seemed, brought out that side of his nature.
'Er—I think maybe you should take a shower or something before you leave,' he advised as she turned to
march determinedly through to the adjoining sitting-
room.

'No, thank you,' she answered tightly, sitting down
to pull on one of her boots, wrinkling her nose delicately because he hadn't quite managed to erase the
smell from the carpet the night before.

'Don't worry about it,' Zak dismissed. 'I'll call
Housekeeping back and get them to shampoo the carpet while I'm out.'

'You know...' she paused to glare up at him, obviously not happy at being reminded of her illness the
evening before '...if you had anything of the gentle-

man about you then you wouldn't have slept in the same bed as me last night!'

'There's only the one bed,' Zak protested, leaning against the doorjamb between the two rooms as he watched her, his arms folded across his chest.

'Then you should have slept on the sofa in here!' she snapped, pulling her second boot on and tying it so tightly Zak was sure it must be cutting off the blood circulating to her foot.

'It happens to be *my* bed,' he reminded her.

'Yes, but—I would have been happier if you had left me on the sofa,' she insisted, standing up.

'Oh, I couldn't have done that,' he assured her mockingly. 'What if you had been sick again? You might have choked on your own—'

'Please don't talk about that any more!' Tyler practically shrieked, picking up from the table all the articles Zak had emptied from her pockets the night before.

'I really think you should take advantage of the bathroom facilities before you leave, Tyler,' Zak reiterated as he once again took in her appearance.

Her eyes flashed as she looked up. 'I don't—oh, no!' she groaned as she caught sight of herself in a mirror, reaching up a hand to her hair as it stood up in the best likeness to an annoyed porcupine Zak had ever seen. 'You could have told me!' she growled as she marched past him into the adjoining bathroom.

'I thought I just did,' he called out over the sound of water running, grinning unabashedly as she came back from the bathroom, her hair now wet and spiky. 'Not much of an improvement, really,' he teased.

'You—' Tyler broke off, drawing in a controlling

breath before speaking again. 'I didn't notice my appearance putting you off a few minutes ago!'

'No. Well, a woman in your bed is worth two that
aren't,' he deliberately misquoted.

Her eyes flashed deeply brown. 'I wouldn't have
thought you were that desperate!'

Zak's smile widened at her attempts to insult him,
easily guessing the reasons behind it—embarrassment,
mainly—but having no intention of helping her out.
The fact that she didn't appear in a very good light
either should be enough to discourage her from writing
about it. *Should* be...

His mouth firmed as he straightened away from the
doorframe. 'I'm sure you'll be relieved to know I'm
not even the slightest bit desperate,' he assured her.
'Now, if you will excuse me, I have to shower and
change before my luncheon appointment.'

'I—of course.' Tyler looked flustered now. 'Can we
meet up again later today?'

'Okay,' he said, wondering now about her personal
life. Did she have parents still alive? Did she have
siblings? Where had she gone to school? Was there a
current man in her life? Those thoughts were immediately followed by the question, why did he want to
know?

He had been forced into agreeing to have Tyler
Wood in his life for a week, and when that week was
over he had no intention of ever setting eyes on her
again. So why should he care about the answer to any
of those questions?

He sighed. 'I've been invited to a party later this
evening, so you may as well come with me.'

'If you're sure I wouldn't be intruding—'

'I thought you were already doing that,' Zak responded with brutal honesty.

Tyler winced. 'I'm sure there must be someone in your life at the moment—'

'If there is I can assure you that you aren't ever going to meet her!' Zak cut in harshly.

'If you resent my being here so much, why did you agree—?' She broke off as he steadily returned her gaze, blond brows raised. 'You didn't agree, did you?' she acknowledged with another wince.

He gave a derisive smile. 'You already know that I didn't.'

Tyler grimaced. 'I thought your initial—lack of co-operation was because I wasn't the man you thought you had agreed to be interviewed by. But now I realize it's much more deep-rooted than that.'

'Much more,' he confirmed grimly. 'Although that doesn't change the fact that the agreement was made, with or without my consent,' he continued as she frowned. 'Now, I suggest you come back to the hotel about eight o'clock this evening. That way I can be sure that you have dinner before we go on to the party. God knows what the speculation would be like if you were to faint halfway through the evening!'

Her cheeks coloured furiously. 'I'm perfectly capable of feeding myself, thank you—'

'Really?' Zak was deeply sceptical. 'I haven't seen much evidence of that so far!'

Her eyes flashed. 'I told you, it was the brandy that made me ill; the fact that I hadn't had dinner yesterday evening had nothing to do with it!' She glared across at him.

His gaze narrowed on her speculatively, taking in the hollows of her cheeks, the slenderness of her body, her wrists so delicately thin they looked as if they might break if any pressure was exerted on them. In fact, Tyler Wood was altogether too slim.

'Tyler, I gave you the brandy because you almost fainted, presumably from lack of food. Which brings us back to the fact that you still haven't told me why you didn't eat dinner yesterday,' he probed.

'There wasn't time.' Once again her gaze seemed to be avoiding meeting his.

Zak didn't buy that explanation; there had been plenty of time for her to eat in between their parting yesterday morning and meeting up again in the evening. Unless she had been expecting him to give her dinner yesterday evening? That would certainly explain why she looked so uncomfortable about the subject...

'Just be back here, and dressed for an evening out, by eight o'clock this evening, Tyler,' he ordered. 'If you're not, then I will have already left without you,' he warned as she would have protested.

She bit down on her bottom lip, looking as if she would like to tell him exactly what he could do with both his dinner and his evening out, but at the same time that impulse obviously warring with the consequences of doing so, namely losing the interview.

Maybe it was a little unfair of him to take advantage of her obvious wish to do the interview, but at the moment, impatient with the situation, puzzled by some of her behaviour, and—yes—frustrated as hell from their passionate kiss earlier on, he wasn't in a mood to be fair!

Worse, he had a distinct feeling this was only the beginning of his feelings of frustration where Tyler Wood was concerned...

CHAPTER FOUR

'WHERE have you been all night? Or need I ask?' Perry scowled at Tyler darkly as he got up from where he had been sitting on the staircase to the next floor of her apartment building.

Tyler frowned, slightly out of breath herself after having just staggered up the two flights of stairs to her apartment. She had been ill last night, didn't feel a hundred per cent now, a fact not enhanced by a journey on the hot and claustrophobic London tube; the last thing she needed at the moment was to be asked about last night. Anything about last night!

'Perry,' she greeted lightly, putting the key in the lock to her apartment and opening the door, at once feeling soothed by the untidy comfort of her sitting-room, the furniture old, the sofa sagging slightly, books taking up every conceivable piece of space. But it was her own little world, nonetheless.

A world she would have preferred to retire to alone, after that second run-in with Zak this morning, in order to lick her wounds in private, if for no other reason. Something she knew wouldn't be possible as, without being invited to do so, Perry followed her inside.

'Tyler, I asked you a quest—'

'Perry,' she cut him off, her look of quiet intensity enough to silence him, for the moment. 'As you can see, I have just got home,' she continued softly, 'so do you think we could possibly delay this conversation until after I've at least showered and changed into some clean clothes?'

Not that she really owed Perry an explanation; no matter what he might wish to the contrary, their relationship had only ever been a working one. But it was that working relationship, and the fact that he had also been hauled over the coals a couple of weeks ago, with the threat of dismissal if they didn't come up with something sensational, pictures included, where Zak Prince was concerned, that made her feel an obligation to him.

'Fine,' he accepted tersely. 'I'll just sit here and wait for you.' He dropped down onto the sagging sofa. 'Tyler, you do know that Zak Prince is—'

'Not now, Perry,' she warned—very much at the end of her tether when it came to the subject of Zak Prince. 'Help yourself to coffee,' she invited before turning in the direction of her bedroom. 'I'll try not to be too long.'

'I'm not going anywhere,' he assured her.

Tyler breathed a sigh of relief once she reached the relative sanctuary of her bedroom, the first time she had really been able to relax since waking up this morning and finding herself in bed with Zak.

In bed with Zak!

Just the memory of that was enough to make her drop down weakly onto her bed.

It was bad enough that she had woken and found herself in bed with him, but it was what had followed that disturbed her the most: Zak Prince very thoroughly kissing her.

And her kissing him right back...

If the woman from Housekeeping hadn't interrupted them when she did...!

Then what?

What did she think would have happened? That the two of them would have carried on making love?

Tyler gave a groan of self-loathing. What a stupid, stupid thing for her to have allowed to happen. Zak had made it more than obvious that he had very little respect for her as a reporter as it was. After she'd fallen into his arms like that, he probably had none at all for her as a woman now, either.

'Tyler?' A knock on the bedroom door accompanied Perry's query. 'Are you all right in there? Only I can't hear the shower running.'

'I'm fine,' she answered sharply, glaring at the closed door. 'But I could be a while, so why don't you—?'

'I'm staying right here, Tyler,' Perry informed her doggedly.

She got wearily to her feet, still frowning her irritation with Perry's badgering as she grabbed some fresh clothes and went through to the adjoining shower-room.

Not that she felt too much better half an hour later, freshly showered and dressed in a clean white tee shirt and faded denims, her hair washed and moussed. All surface dressing in an effort to boost her bruised morale, knowing that, after what had happened between them this morning, Zak was going to be more obnoxious that ever when she met up with him this evening.

And she still had a disgruntled Perry sitting in her lounge!

'Coffee?' she offered as she came through from the bedroom and saw that he hadn't made himself a cup after all.

'No, thanks,' he refused tersely, standing up. 'I re-

ally wasn't exaggerating, was I, when I said Zak
Prince can't be alone with a woman for five minutes
without trying to seduce her into his bed? Only in your
case it doesn't seem to have taken even five minutes!'
He looked at her scornfully.

Tyler felt the colour drain from her cheeks. 'Perry,
you have absolutely no right—'

'No right!' he exclaimed, shaking his head in disgust. 'Tyler, I stood outside the hotel last night for
over five hours waiting for one or both of you to come
out. Then I tried calling you when I got home. Then
again at two o'clock. Then again at six o'clock this
morning.' His mouth twisted derisively. 'The fact that
you were still wearing your clothes from yesterday
when you arrived home, and looked as if you had just
fallen out of bed—literally!—is more than enough reason for me to have added two and two together and
come up with the appropriate answer of four!
Wouldn't you say?' His eyes glittered with accusation.

Tyler drew in a sharp breath. It was probably as
well Perry hadn't been inside the hotel when Zak had
swept her up in his arms and carried her away to his
hotel suite! 'Perry, I think you had better leave before
you say anything else you're going to regret,' she
warned.

He dismissed the warning with a wave of his hand.
'Is that all you have to say to me? Tyler, I thought the
two of us meant something to each other. As friends,
if nothing else,' he added as she would have argued
that point.

'Oh, Perry, of course we're friends.' She groaned.
'But nothing happened between Zak Prince and me
last night,' she told him heavily, knowing that wasn't
quite true of this morning, but having no intention of

sharing that humiliation with anyone—including Perry.

'I hope for your sake that it didn't,' he snapped. 'We're supposed to be digging up the dirt on Zak Prince—I would hate for you to be part of it!'

That was the choice her editor had given her after Tyler had effectively blown the story on Jinx Nixon; deliver as much scandal on Zak Prince as she could, or else she could look for another job. Having walked out on her home and family six months ago with the brave declaration she was perfectly capable of making it on her own, she had no intention of getting fired from her very first job as a reporter.

Although that didn't stop her inwardly cringing at the knowledge that this interview with Zak was intended as lurid fodder for the tabloids, rather than the restrained Sunday magazine supplement article that she had told Zak it would be. This type of journalism was not exactly what she had had in mind when she'd made those grand announcements to her family!

'I was ill last night, and Zak Prince was kind enough—'

'You were ill?' Perry moved to her side to look down at her with concern. 'What happened? Why were you ill? Do you need to see a doctor?'

A head doctor, maybe—for being stupid enough not to have rebuffed Zak this morning when he'd kissed her!

'No.' She gave a humourless laugh. 'I don't need to see a doctor. I—inadvertently drank some brandy—'

'Oh, no,' Perry groaned in sympathy, well aware of her allergy to alcohol. 'But how on earth—?'

'It was an accident, okay?' she told him sharply. 'I

drank it. I was ill. And Zak Prince took care of me. End of story.' As far as explaining herself to Perry it was, but she had a definite feeling that Zak would have other ideas on the subject!

'You poor love,' Perry sympathized. 'And all I did when you finally managed to stagger home was hurl accusations at you. Will you let me make you some coffee to make up for my boorish behaviour?'

'Fine,' she accepted as she dropped down into an armchair, just wanting to forget this awkwardness between them; goodness knew she had made few enough friends since moving to London without alienating Perry too. And she really didn't need any more confrontation—she was only just starting to feel a little better.

Although, she had to admit, the thought of meeting Zak Prince again at eight o'clock this evening was enough to make her feel ill all over again!

'You're looking good,' Zak complimented her as he opened the door to his hotel suite at exactly eight o'clock that evening and saw a transformed Tyler standing outside.

She did look good. Very good, in fact. The red dress she wore clung in all the right places as it emphasized pert breasts and the curve of her hips—she was obviously wearing very little clothing underneath the figure-hugging dress. Its above-knee length showed off a long expanse of shapely tanned legs, and the high heels on the matching red shoes she wore added a good three inches to her diminutive height.

His practised eye told him she was wearing more make-up than usual too—those dark lashes surrounding her huge brown eyes looking longer and silkier than ever, a delicate blush emphasizing her cheek-bones, and a red gloss on her lips adding to their full-ness.

'Dressed for battle, hmm?' he guessed.

'A party, I thought,' she came back lightly as she walked past him into the suite.

Zak grinned appreciatively as he turned to watch the sway of her hips. He hadn't been quite sure what to expect when Tyler arrived this evening—the spitfire of their first and second meeting, or the young woman this morning who had seemed confused and not a little upset at their response to each other in bed; he certainly hadn't been expecting this beautiful siren. She had obviously sat back when she'd got home earlier, regrouped, and this dynamically beautiful woman was the result.

'You're looking pretty good yourself,' she returned the compliment as her gaze travelled slowly up the length of his body.

Zak frowned, finding he was uncomfortable with the way Tyler had looked at him with such feminine assessment as she took in his appearance in the cream silk shirt and brown trousers he wore this evening. As he had looked at her own changed appearance seconds ago in the red dress with complete male assessment…? Hell, yes, but— But nothing. What was good enough for him, her challenging gaze now said, was good enough for her, too.

There was more, much more, it seemed, to Tyler Wood than he had at first given her credit for…

'Thanks,' he accepted as casually as he could. 'I won't bother to offer you a drink before we leave— we both know where *that* could lead!' he taunted, blue eyes challenging *her* now.

Tyler didn't even blink at his deliberate reminder of last night and this morning. 'You mentioned that we would be having dinner before the party…?'

'O'Malley's.' He nodded. 'If that's okay with you?'

'Oh, I think I'll be able to cope,' she said dryly.

The restaurant he had chosen was the in-place at the moment, a cross between an Irish pub and a superb English-cuisine restaurant. But, despite what Tyler might think to the contrary, that wasn't the reason Zak had chosen it. O'Malley's was more relaxed than the other fashionable London eateries, and Zak didn't particularly enjoy dining in formal restaurants. From the brief time he had spent in Tyler's company, he hadn't thought she would either, but her appearance this evening told him very firmly that she would be comfortable no matter what her surroundings.

'Good,' he said as he opened the door for her to leave, still feeling strangely wrong-footed by this stunning woman—something that didn't happen to him too often, he had to admit.

He caught a faint whiff of her perfume as she moved smoothly past him out into the corridor, a heady mixture of clean flesh and that elusively floral concoction.

Tyler was most definitely not his type, he told himself firmly as he accompanied her to the lift. For one thing he abhorred short hair on a woman—he couldn't stand that almost as much as the unfeminine combat trousers Tyler had worn yesterday. Worst of all, she was that loathed of all things, a reporter!

Then why, if he disliked all those things about her, had the memory of her this morning, soft and pliant in his arms, her body warm and inviting, been intruding into his thoughts all day?

'Are you okay?'

He turned sharply at her huskily spoken query. 'Why shouldn't I be?'

'No reason.' Tyler shrugged. 'It's just that the elevator has stopped at the ground floor and you don't seem to want to get out…?'

The lift had indeed stopped at the ground floor. Several people were standing outside waiting to get in, although the recognition in their eyes as they looked at him seemed to say they were in no particular hurry for him to leave.

'Sorry.' His smile of apology encompassed them all as he took a firm hold of Tyler's elbow to step out into the reception area, keeping a hold of her arm as they walked over to the doors at the front of this sumptuously elegant building.

'Are you sure you're okay?' Tyler repeated once they were seated in the cab on the way to the restaurant.

No, he wasn't sure he was okay! Women came and went in his life, with rapidity, if the recent comments of his two brothers were anything to go by, and while he enjoyed their company—and other things!—for the duration of the relationship, he never gave any of those women a second thought once the relationship came to an end. In fact, he had found himself thinking more about Tyler in the last twenty-four hours than he had about any of those women. He could still feel the softness of her skin beneath his hands, the inviting warmth of her lips beneath his.

It was because they weren't in a relationship, he told himself firmly. It was just frustrated lust, that was all. And it was because he had to be careful what he said and did around Tyler—otherwise he might just find that the result of being incautious was being plastered across the front page of a tabloid newspaper.

'I really am fine,' he assured her confidently, glad he had sorted that particular problem out in his mind. 'What have you done with your day?' he changed the subject promptly.

'Done with my day?' she echoed sharply. 'What on earth should I have done with it?'

Zak gave her a quizzical smile. 'I'm just making conversation, Tyler.'

'Oh.' She looked uncomfortable now, her gaze not quite meeting his, her previous air of confidence starting to look a little shaky. 'Well, I—I tidied my apartment, if you really want to know.'

His mouth quirked upwards a little. 'Very domesticated,' he teased, thinking of the complete disarray they had just left behind in his hotel suite. 'Do you live alone?'

'Yes—I live alone!' she snapped. 'Although I can't imagine what business that is of yours.'

Neither could he, if the truth were known, but for some reason he had been curious to know whether she lived with her boyfriend, Perry Morgan. The latter could have proved a little embarrassing considering her non-appearance at home last night!

'Besides,' she continued firmly, 'I'm the one who's supposed to ask *you* the questions.'

'I was just showing an interest, Tyler, attempting to get to know you a little better.'

'Well, I would prefer it if you didn't,' she told him tartly.

Obviously, Zak noted. 'That hardly seems fair when you already know so much about me.'

'Mr Prince—Zak,' she corrected as he raised mocking brows, 'your life is an open book—anyone and everyone can read about it!—and that's the life you chose. Whereas I chose—'

'To be one of those who exposes other people's lives,' he gibed. 'While keeping your own life completely private.'

She shrugged. 'That's my prerogative.'

He turned on the bench seat to look at her, his arm resting along the back behind her. 'And if *I* want to know more about *you*?' His hand moved to rest on her shoulder now, his fingers gently caressing behind the lobe of her ear.

The air in the back of the taxi was so tense between them that it seemed to literally hang there, so thick it felt as if it held them within a cocoon of—of what? Zak wasn't sure. And for the moment he didn't particularly care, either, all of his attention focused on Tyler. On how addictive her kisses were. On how he wanted to caress her breasts again so badly that—

'Zak, are you playing some sort of game with me?' She interrupted his unwittingly lustful imaginings with her question. 'Look, I know I made a bit of an idiot of myself last night—okay, a big idiot of myself last night—being so ill,' she corrected herself. 'But that doesn't give you the right to—to—?'

'Yes?' he prompted huskily, barely able to repress his smile at her obvious feelings of awkwardness over last night. Even if his own thoughts did run more to what had happened this morning rather than last night!

She spotted his smile. '*You* gave me the brandy!' she reminded him indignantly.

Yes, he had, and he really hadn't enjoyed seeing the way it had made her so ill. He just couldn't find it in himself to really regret holding her in his arms this morning...

'How was I to know the effect it would have on you?' he reasoned.

'You weren't,' she acknowledged with a sigh. 'But that's still no reason for you to assume that we—'

'Yes?' he asked, utterly fascinated by the way she always hesitated when it came to mentioning anything about sex—and especially the sexual attraction that existed between the two of them.

Why was that? he wondered. Most of the time Tyler was the confident, accomplished woman that she obviously was, but at the mere mention of anything sexual she seemed to shy away, as if she were embarrassed by the subject. Almost as if—

'You aren't gay, are you?' he wanted to know. Now that would bring a smile to his brothers' faces: Zak having been to bed with a woman who wasn't even interested in men!

'Did it seem that way this morning?' Tyler asked, outraged. 'But even if I were, I don't see why it should be any of your business,' she added hurriedly, instantly regretting mentioning what had happened that morning.

He didn't think it was any of his business either. Not really. Because, no matter how tempted he was, and no matter how much time he had to spend with her over the next week, he had firmly decided that he had no intention of taking the sexual attraction he felt towards her any further than he already had. If he wasn't careful, that would become the story!

'Good point,' he accepted, moving back to his own side of the bench seat. 'Although it could have given you an interesting slant on what you choose to write about me.'

Tyler gave a dismissive snort. 'So far I haven't found anything to write about you that hasn't already been said!'

'Good,' he said with satisfaction, his gaze narrowing slightly as he sensed a certain disappointment in her tone. 'You know, Tyler, maybe you chose the wrong brother to write about. Nik isn't of much interest now that he's married and settled down, but I have a feeling that you would find Rik's reserve hides something much more interesting than anything you will learn about me!'

'At this particular moment I would find Donald Duck more interesting than you,' she jeered.

'Then I suggest you consider writing something about him—because I guarantee you are going to learn absolutely nothing new about me to interest your readership!'

Zak hadn't realized how angry he was about being pressured into this until he started talking about it.

Or had this depth of anger only arisen since he had actually met Tyler and realized how attractive she was?

Oh, he had been angry with the press before, but his anger was usually directed towards the media in general, at the way it seemed any of them would do anything, use any method, to obtain a story. But since Zak had met Tyler, that anger had become much more personal.

In fact, he realized, he found the idea of her, in particular, using such methods to obtain a story more than a little distasteful and incredibly disappointing.

Although he had no idea what that meant!

CHAPTER FIVE

'TYLER...? My God, Tyler, is that really you?'

Having only arrived at O'Malley's a few minutes previously, Tyler was in the process of sitting down at their table when she immediately stood up again and froze, almost afraid to turn around and look at the person who had just spoken to her.

Because she had instantly recognized that precise English voice. And it belonged to someone who knew more about her than she wanted Zak to know!

'It *is* you!' Gerald Knight suddenly popped up in front of her. 'Darling!' He grabbed hold of her and held her at arm's length. 'You've lost so much weight I hardly recognized you! And the short hair is gorgeous!' He beamed at her before kissing her on both cheeks. 'How long have you been in England, you naughty girl?'

'Several months,' she answered.

'And you haven't called me?' He gave her a look of affectionate reproval. 'Shame on you!'

He released Tyler just in time for her to turn and see the expression on Zak's face as he looked at the other man.

Her hackles instantly rose in Gerald's defence, knowing that his rather effeminate manner was just something he had developed over years of working exclusively with women.

Despite this, she still wished she hadn't bumped into Gerald this evening, swiftly realizing she had no choice but to introduce the two men. 'Gerald Knight, this is—'

'The actor, Zak Prince,' Gerald finished, at the same time shaking the other man's hand enthusiastically.

'Gerald Knight, the fashion designer?' Zak said slowly as he released Gerald's hand.

'You've heard of me!' Gerald beamed with delight even as his professionally critical gaze took in Zak's clothing. Short and slim himself, Gerald always designed and wore his own suits and shirts, and was dressed in a brown suit this evening, matched with the palest of pink shirts.

Tyler had no doubts that Zak's clothes boasted a label of similar pedigree, but he somehow still managed to look casually untidy against Gerald's dapperness.

'But of course,' Zak answered the other man. 'Your New York shows are always worth going to.'

Gerald threw back his head and gave one of his hearty chuckles, prompting several other diners to turn and look curiously at the standing trio. 'Naughty, naughty,' he reproved Zak teasingly. 'Those clothes aren't designed for men to ogle.'

'No?' Zak raised a mocking eyebrow. 'Does that mean I've been wrong all these years in assuming a woman dressed with the intention of looking good for men?'

'Totally wrong. Women dress to impress other women. And may I say, darling Tyler, that I'm very disappointed in you for wearing a Vera Wang. What's wrong with a Gerald Knight? Especially now that you've lost all that baby fat,' Gerald continued admiringly. 'You're looking absolutely marvellous. I had no idea there was this fantastic figure underneath all that—'

It was round about here that Tyler stopped listening and concentrated on what Zak must be thinking instead. She was dreading the questions that must surely follow Gerald's rather tactless remarks!

'Earth to Tyler.' Gerald's face suddenly appeared in her vision as he bent down to waggle his eyebrows at her. 'Hello—anyone home?'

'Sorry, Gerald.' She dragged her attention back from a slightly dazed-looking Zak. 'What were you saying?' She forced a bright smile of interest.

'I said how does Rufus feel about the new you? And the new boyfriend, of course,' he asked suggestively.

Tyler's eyes widened, not just at the mention of Rufus, but at Gerald's assumption that Zak was her boyfriend! She might even have laughed at the idea— if she hadn't thought it would turn into a hysterical cackle!

'Oops, got to go,' Gerald announced suddenly after a quick glance at the gold Rolex on his wrist. 'I should have been at the theatre fifteen minutes ago. Oh, well, never mind; I'm sure they've started without me! Now, Tyler, how much longer are you in London? Do call me, darling. We must meet up for lunch and have a really good natter. Must dash! Bye, Zak.' And with a brief wave of one slightly limp hand he disappeared out of the restaurant.

Leaving absolute chaos in his charming wake as far as Tyler was concerned! She sank down weakly into her seat, feeling a little as if she had just been run over by an express train. She didn't dare so much as glance at Zak to see how *he* was feeling!

What had Gerald said exactly? Tyler fretted.

Well, he had easily recognized her dress as a Vera Wang, for one thing. How many rookie reporters could afford to buy a Vera Wang?

Gerald had also made the erroneous assumption concerning her relationship with Zak.

And, worst of all, he had mentioned Rufus...

In fact, none of it had been good!

'Whew,' Zak breathed heavily as he sat down opposite her. 'Is he always like that?'

'Always,' she said ruefully. 'A little of Gerald tends to go a long way, if you know what I mean?'

'Oh, I know exactly what you mean! So how come you and Gerald Knight are such old friends?'

'Oh, I wouldn't go that far,' she dismissed airily, looking up to smile her thanks at the waiter as he handed her a menu.

'No, thanks,' Zak refused his menu. 'I'll have the garlic king prawns to start, followed by the duck—'

'I'm afraid the menu was changed last week, sir, and the duck is no longer on it,' the waiter said apologetically. 'But I can recommend the pheasant—'

'I don't like pheasant,' Zak cut in sharply.

'Then perhaps the—'

'I'll have a steak, medium to rare, with a green salad, and a side order of fries,' Zak almost barked the order out.

Tyler listened to the exchange with interest; admittedly Zak had been rude to her from the beginning, but she hadn't seen or heard him be anything but charming with everyone else. Including the doorman at the hotel, the cab driver on the way over here, and the man who had shown them to their table. He had even been pleasant to the often overwhelming Gerald.

So why was he being such a pain in the butt to this

waiter, especially when the problem wasn't even the guy's fault? She gave her order—the garlic prawns like Zak, but followed by the baked sea bass—in a carefully polite voice and accompanied by a smile, to make up for Zak's curtness.

Zak turned back as the waiter disappeared with their order. 'I had my heart set on the duck, okay?' he muttered as he saw Tyler's questioning look.

'Yeah. Right.' Tyler turned away, looking around at the other diners, most of them easily recognizable, either from the big or small screen.

'Tyler?'

She took her time responding, trying to get her disappointment under control. Because she was deeply disappointed with Zak. Okay, she was supposed to write as scandalous an article on this man as she could, but a part of her was secretly hoping there wouldn't be any scandal to write about.

Even if she then lost her job?

Even then, she acknowledged heavily. Because, despite the way he behaved towards her, she actually liked Zak Prince.

His resentment towards her and the methods she had used to obtain this week-long interview with him were understandable, she had decided earlier as she'd got ready for their evening out. But his behaviour just now, to a man who was only doing his job—and was probably only getting paid peanuts to do it, too!—she hadn't liked at all.

'I really wanted the duck, okay,' he repeated at her continued silence.

'I already said it was okay,' she dismissed.

'No, what you actually said—'

'Zak,' she interrupted quietly, 'why should it matter

what I did or didn't say? We're a reporter—an un-wanted one, at that!—and an actor, out to dinner, not some long-married couple who are answerable to each other for their actions!' She didn't really want to go any further with this subject—although there was def-initely a bonus to it; while they were talking about Zak, it kept the conversation away from their encoun-ter with Gerald Knight!

Zak drew in a sharp breath, his expression remote. 'You're right, it doesn't matter.'

But it obviously did. To him. He seemed incredibly uncomfortable with her—or anyone else?—thinking badly of him. Interesting...

'I should go easy on the red meat, though, if I were you.' She eyed him mockingly over the rim of her glass as she sipped from the glass of sparkling water she had ordered to accompany her meal. 'It may make you even more aggressive.'

'I am *not*—' He broke off, his gaze narrowing on her speculatively. 'You're deliberately trying to irritate me now, aren't you?'

Tyler opened wide innocent eyes. 'Would I?'

'Oh, yes.' Zak began to smile. 'I keep underesti-mating you, don't I?'

'Do you?' She maintained her innocent expression.

'Yeah.' Zak was openly grinning now. 'But luckily I've just realized why.'

'You have?'

He gave a rueful shake of his head. 'I'll grant that you did succeed in diverting my attention for a while there, but not indefinitely, unfortunately for you.'

Damn!

Tyler kept her own smile on her lips. 'No?' she retorted mildly.

'No,' he confirmed. 'You were hoping that I would be diverted enough to forget all about asking for an explanation as to how you know a fashion designer of Gerald Knight's acclaim. Or exactly who Rufus is. And just how—large you were the last time Gerald saw you. Let me also assure you, there is no way you wouldn't be noticed in that spectacular dress—Vera Wang, or otherwise!'

There was also the fact, Tyler thought semi-hysterically, that he hadn't noticed Perry getting out of a cab just behind theirs when they'd arrived at the restaurant a short time ago, and that the other man was still lurking about outside somewhere, hoping he might get a photograph or two when they left!

'Well?' Zak prompted expectantly as no answer was forthcoming on any of the three statements he had just made.

Tyler was certainly turning out to be more of a surprise than he could possibly have realized before actually meeting her—and he was no longer just referring to the fact that she had turned out to be female!

He had known that she looked good when she'd arrived at the hotel earlier, couldn't help but notice how the red dress clung in all the right places. Though, not being interested in clothes himself, he couldn't tell a designer dress from one bought in a high-street store!

But it had been totally obvious that Tyler and Gerald Knight were old friends from way back, that the man knew her well.

And just who the hell was Rufus? An old boy-friend? A current boyfriend, even! Her brother? Just another friend? Although Gerald's remarks certainly hadn't seemed to imply the relationship was anything that casual.

Although why should he care one way or the other when Tyler was nothing but a nuisance of a reporter who had bargained her way into his life?

Because, Zak realized unwillingly, she had stopped being just a nuisance reporter this morning, when he'd taken her in his arms and kissed her...

'Well what?' Tyler finally replied, not even looking up at him, her attention on the pattern she was tracing on the frosted outside of her glass of mineral water. She only glanced up when Zak didn't respond and simply continued to watch her.

Tyler seemed to think quickly and finally offered an explanation. 'Gerald and I met some time ago in New York when I did a feature on one of his fashion shows. For some reason he took a liking to me and we've been friends ever since.'

Zak could quite easily see how that had happened— he was starting to like her himself. Which was the worst thing he could do, considering who and what she was.

Maybe if he tried to picture a much larger Tyler...? No, that wasn't going to work; he thought Tyler was far too thin now and could do with putting on ten pounds or so. The fact that Gerald Knight, a man who surrounded himself with wafer-thin models, had found Tyler's new slenderness attractive was enough to confirm that opinion.

Besides, thin or slightly fuller in the figure, she would still have those melting chocolate-brown eyes, and the more time Zak spent in her company, the more he liked her mischievous sense of humour.

But there was still the question of Rufus...

'And what about Rufus?' Zak raised blond brows. 'Did he take a liking to you too?'

Those chocolate-brown eyes suddenly filled with tears, only to be rapidly blinked away as Tyler's expression changed to one of anger. 'I wouldn't know—the two of us haven't spoken for six months!' she snapped.

Quite what Zak would have said next, he had no idea, but their first course had arrived to be placed on the table in front of them. 'Thanks.' He gave the waiter a warm smile, not at all happy with himself at having snapped at the man earlier. As Tyler clearly hadn't been either.

Zak had his reasons for reacting to the menu change in the way that he had. But he had no intention of explaining those reasons to Tyler. They were private and not to be splashed over the tabloid papers!

The waiter's obviously relieved, 'You're welcome,' didn't make Zak feel any less uncomfortable with his earlier behaviour.

Neither did glancing across the table and seeing the derisive expression on Tyler's face.

'Does that smile usually work?' she asked.

Zak instantly lost his appetite for the king prawns they were both eating. Yes, that smile usually succeeded in making up for any slight he might have given when under stress. As he had been earlier...

'I made a mistake,' he admitted. 'I'm sure even you must make them on occasion?'

'Frequently,' she replied. 'But I hope I'm usually big enough to apologize for them.'

Damn it, she knew nothing about him, had no idea what might have been the reason for his earlier bad humour. And considering the way she had pushed herself into his life, she certainly had no right to lecture him on his behaviour. She—

'I hope you're enjoying your meal, sir, madam.' The waiter had returned to place two bowls of warm lemon water and two napkins on the table for them to use to clean their hands after eating their prawns.

Zak shot Tyler a narrow-eyed glare before turning back to the waiter. 'I'm sorry if I seemed—abrupt, concerning the duck earlier. I shouldn't have taken my disappointment out on you.'

'Please think nothing of it, Mr Prince,' the middle-aged man assured him. 'Your reaction to the change of menu was mild in comparison to the lady last week who threw her glass of wine over me when I broke the news to her! I've mentioned the two incidents to the chef, and I believe he is even now considering putting the duck back on the menu.' There was a definite twinkle in his eyes as he departed to let them finish their starters.

Zak glanced triumphantly across at Tyler, his eyes widening with suspicion as he saw she was desperately biting her bottom lip in an effort not to laugh. But those mischievous brown eyes gave her away. 'Are you laughing at me?' he exclaimed.

'No—but I'm going to!' She burst out laughing, not the soft, affected laughter he heard so often from other famous people, but a deep-throated chuckle that owed nothing to soft and everything to earthy.

Her eyes sparkled, her creamy cheeks glowed, her smile was radiant; in fact, she looked beautiful.

And Zak wasn't the only man in the restaurant to think so, either.

Several male heads turned in their direction, most of them known to Zak, some of them friends of his. Although not such good friends he would welcome them coming over to say hello, his warning expression clearly told them.

Tyler finally stopped laughing to give a rueful shake of her head. 'I have no doubts that the menu will quickly be adjusted to include the duck! You really can be incredibly charming when you want to be, can't you?' she said with unhidden admiration.

He grimaced. 'Meaning I haven't succeeded in being so too often around you!'

She shrugged, still smiling. 'I did say when you *wanted* to be...'

And he hadn't wanted to be around Tyler. He still didn't. She was just too dangerous, too much in his face. It was better if she wrote that he wasn't always as charmingly relaxed as previously reported than she root out the makings of a real story on him.

Not that it was anything he was ashamed of; it just wasn't something he had ever talked about in public. He'd had problems as a child, and had rebelled as a teenager because of those childhood difficulties. He had managed to put things behind him after he'd attained success as an actor, and it was only sometimes, like this evening, that the difficulties once again raised their head.

Nik had told him he should have come clean years ago, but the longer Zak left it, the harder it became to talk about something so personal to him. And he certainly didn't want it splashed all over the tabloid rag Tyler worked for!

'As my mother used to say—eat your prawns,' he muttered gruffly as he picked up one of the prawns on his own plate and began to take the shell off.

Tyler's brows rose incredulously. 'Your mother used to say that a lot, did she?'

'I think it was usually in reference to vegetables or salad.' Zak shrugged. 'But the principle is the same.'

'Shut up and eat?'

'You got it,' he drawled.

CHAPTER SIX

As THEY continued with the rest of their meal Tyler was relieved to have succeeded in diverting Zak's attention away from the subject of Rufus, and what he meant to her.

Momentarily, that was.

Because she had no doubts that Zak would return to the subject when he felt so inclined. She would just have to make sure she had a suitable answer ready for him when he did.

Quite what, she had no idea yet—the truth simply wouldn't do on this occasion.

This was all getting so complicated!

It had all seemed so simple when she had initially made her decision to come to England and make a success of herself as a reporter. All she'd had to do was find somewhere to live, get a job with a newspaper, and then write a sensational story that would make her name known on both sides of the Atlantic. Then she could go home in triumph.

Well, she had come over here, found herself an apartment and a job—but when the 'sensational' story had presented itself to her in the form of revealing Jinx Nixon's connection to the famous writer J. I. Watson, she had made a complete hash of it!

It had been mainly due, she knew, to that tendency to become emotionally involved that Zak had mentioned earlier today. Nik Prince had appealed to her finer instincts and asked her not to write the story on

Jinx, and like an idiot she had given up her first chance at success.

Something she simply couldn't do a second time where Zak Prince was concerned!

She had wanted to be a reporter ever since she could remember—except in her family you didn't work for a newspaper or a television station. You might own them, and pay other people to work in them, but you certainly didn't work there yourself.

As an only child of extremely wealthy parents, she had pretty well had her life mapped out for her before she could even talk—the right school, the right college, the right friends—and then some time helping her mother to run their numerous homes and the many charities she was involved in, before meeting the right man, marrying him, and starting the process all over again with her own children.

In a word, her life had been massively constricted.

But it had been her parents' choice of husband for her six months ago that had made Tyler finally decide that enough was enough—and she had just packed her bags and walked out, her flight to England booked that same day.

And everything had been on schedule for her to succeed in her plans until she'd met the Prince family!

'Did you know you get tiny lines between your eyes when you frown like that?' Zak murmured, obviously having been watching her for some time if his relaxed pose was anything to go by.

Tyler shot him a fiery glance. 'Everyone gets lines between their eyes when they frown!'

'True. I was actually wondering what had caused you to frown…'

'Nothing that need concern you.'

'Fair enough.' He shrugged. 'If you've finished your main course, I suggest we leave.'

'Don't you want dessert?' She held out the menu that the waiter had given her a few minutes ago, for him to look at.

Zak didn't even glance at it. 'I never eat dessert. But you go ahead,' he invited at her look of disappointment.

'No.' She put the menu reluctantly to one side; she loved dessert. 'I wouldn't want to regain all that *baby fat* of mine!'

Zak grinned across the table at her. 'You never did tell me how much larger you once were...'

No—and she hadn't meant to remind him of Gerald's conversation, either. 'A dress size or so—okay, two dress sizes,' she admitted as Zak raised sceptical blond brows. 'But I never had any complaints.' She looked at him challengingly.

He held up placating hands. 'You aren't getting any now, either.'

Tyler gave him a confused look, unsure whether he was flirting with her or not.

'Exactly whose party is it we're going to?' Tyler voiced her curiosity a few minutes later as they made their way out of the restaurant.

'Calum McQuire's.'

'*Calum McQuire's!*' Tyler practically squealed, grabbing his arm in sheer excitement. 'I've always wanted—' She broke off as she saw the pitying look on Zak's face. 'I sound like a kid still in high school, don't I?'

'You do,' Zak confirmed with a grin. 'Although it's good to know you aren't so used to your sophisticated friends that you wouldn't be impressed at the thought of meeting Calum.'

Her eyes widened. 'No one could *not* be impressed at meeting him! Calum McQuire has defined the meaning of the word "private". No one, and I really mean no one, gets to meet him, or his family, if he doesn't want them to.'

In fact, the Scottish actor guarded his privacy so well that he hadn't given an interview, or so much as spoken to a member of the media, in the five years since his son had been born. And Zak was taking her to meet him! Maybe this would turn out to be the exclusive she needed…

'Don't even *think* about it, Tyler,' Zak growled, coming to a halt outside on the pavement as he accurately read her thoughts. 'You will be there as my guest, and I advise you not to abuse the privilege.'

He might not have actually voiced the words, but the threat was there in his voice, anyway: take advantage of the meeting this evening with Calum McQuire, and Zak would make sure every other door was closed to her—indefinitely.

Damn it, she was getting a little tired of people threatening her. First her editor on *The Daily Informer*, Bill Graham, and now Zak was getting in on the act.

Pretty soon she was going to lose her cool at being told what to do all the time, and then they had all better stand well back!

But not tonight, she realized, holding her disappointment in check. Calum McQuire, although media-shy, was supposed to be a nice guy who just wanted his wife and son left out of the limelight that followed him around, to allow his son to have as normal a childhood as possible.

Tyler could relate to that!

She gave Zak a bright smile. 'You can count on my discretion,' she assured him as she turned to go.

His hand on her arm held her beside him. 'Look on this as a test of faith.'

'The man is a movie icon, Zak.' Tyler glared up at him indignantly. 'Everyone loves him. God, when I was a teenager, even I used to fantasize—' She broke off awkwardly. She was doing it again: giving him too much information!

'You "used to fantasize"…?' he prompted with interest.

Tyler felt the colour warm her cheeks. Not because she had admitted to fantasizing about someone that all the girls of her school had had a thing about, but because the comment had reminded her all too forcibly that she had used to fantasize about Zak too…

'I was fifteen, okay!' she protested, turning away, glancing around surreptitiously for Perry now; while she had been inside enjoying the best meal she had eaten in six months, he had been standing outside here probably having had nothing to eat at all.

But she knew from Zak's comments that there was no way Perry was going to get into Calum McQuire's, so maybe she should try and signal to him in some way to let him know he would be wasting his time following them any further, that he might as well go and get something to eat himself.

But even though she sensed that Perry was outside somewhere, she couldn't actually see him. That was the whole point, of course, but even so—

'Have you lost something?'

Tyler turned guiltily at Zak's softly spoken query, her eyes widening as she found herself almost nose to nose with him as he bent his head towards her. It wasn't easy to be so close to him when seconds ago she had been remembering those girlhood fantasies about him.

But she had been a child then. She was a woman of twenty-six now. Except she still wanted him to kiss her...!

She had been fighting this ever since she'd first gone to Zak's hotel suite yesterday morning. No—even before that. Ever since the moment Nik Prince had offered her the deal that entailed her backing off Jinx's story and accepting an exclusive with his brother instead.

She had known at the time that she shouldn't do it, that she was probably committing professional suicide, but the temptation to not only meet Zak Prince, but to spend a whole week in his company, had just been too much for her to resist.

Because there was something she had been keeping from Nik Prince, Bill Graham, Perry, even Zak himself—especially Zak! Her girlhood dreams about this man had never really left her...

When she had been ill in front of Zak last night she had just wanted to die. When he had kissed her this morning she had thought she had died—and gone to heaven!

She had tried so hard to be professional with this man. Had tried to leave her attraction towards him in the past where it belonged—and, to be completely honest, Zak had been so rude and mocking most of the time that she hadn't had too much trouble resisting him. But tonight he seemed less the movie star and more the man behind the image, and, as such, much more approachable.

Considering the major crush she had had on him in her teens, that probably wasn't a good idea. Despite how it might have appeared to Zak at the hotel yesterday morning, she probably knew almost as much about him as his brothers did. Because, as well as covering her bedroom walls with pictures of him, she had collected articles on every interview he had ever given, and had virtually been a walking encyclopaedia on him. Depressingly, she probably still was...

So it totally wasn't a good idea to find herself standing only centimetres away from him, their gazes locked, their breaths shallow and intermingled.

Every inch of her body felt alive, and all her senses were acutely aware of Zak—of the silky softness of that overlong blond hair, the deep, deep blue of his eyes, and his beautifully sculptured mouth, with its sensuous lower lip.

How she longed to kiss that mouth, to run her tongue over his sensuous lips, to taste him, and to feel the strength of his shoulders beneath her hands as she strained against him, to know the—

Tyler blinked dazedly as a bright light suddenly split the darkness, momentarily blinding her.

'What the *hell* was that?' Zak's voice was grim as he turned in the direction the light had come from. But now there was just darkness, only the sound of a car door slamming, quickly followed by the starting of an engine, to show that the incident had happened at all.

It must have been Perry making a hasty getaway after taking their photograph, Tyler realized with dismay as Zak turned back to her, his expression fiercely angry. She took a hasty step back as she saw the murderous glitter of his eyes.

Zak was so furious at what had just happened, and

felt so utterly betrayed after the lively dinner he had just shared with Tyler, that he was almost prepared to strangle her!

'You set that up!' he accused her. 'You deliberately, *calculatingly*, arranged for that photographer—probably your boyfriend Perry—'

'He *isn't* my boyfriend,' she denied. 'And don't be ridiculous. How could I possibly have—?'

'You set *me* up!' At that moment Zak was too angry to listen to anything she might have to say. 'No doubt a photograph of you looking up at me all dewy-eyed and dreamy will appear in tomorrow's newspaper—'

'I was *not* looking at you all dewy-eyed!' Tyler gasped, her face pale in the moonlight.

'Your eyes were begging for me to kiss you,' he jeered.

'They most certainly were not!' she insisted indignantly. '*You* were the one about to kiss *me*—'

'In your dreams!' Zak scorned—knowing even as he said it that he was lying, to himself as well as Tyler.

He *had* been about to kiss her. Had been longing to kiss her all evening. Even when he'd been verbally holding her at arm's length. Even when he'd been angry with her.

She looked absolutely wonderful in that red dress, even her cropped spiky hair no longer the turn off it had been. And as for those melting brown eyes...!

But she had flinched back at his last comment, those dark eyes huge in the otherwise paleness of her face. 'I'm sorry to disappoint you, Zak,' she snapped. 'But no way have you ever featured in any of my dreams!'

He hadn't meant it literally, damn it. He was just so livid with her, and that photographer, that—

'Tyler Wood?'

Zak turned irritably to glare at the woman who had just got out of the cab that had pulled up outside the restaurant. A woman who looked vaguely familiar to him, although for the moment he couldn't place where he had seen the tall, very slender blonde before. He did know he wasn't at all pleased by her interruption.

Tyler didn't look too thrilled at seeing the other woman either, her expression becoming positively guarded even as she took a step backwards.

Zak's gaze narrowed as Tyler gave him a quick glance, before licking her lips and hastily turning away again.

He looked at the blonde once more, eyeing her suspiciously now, knowing by Tyler's behaviour that she wished herself far away from here. And from the sudden widening of the other woman's eyes as she obviously recognized Zak, she was surprised to see whom Tyler was with too.

Who the hell was she? he wondered. Another reporter? That would certainly explain his own feeling of having seen the other woman before. And yet he couldn't think, if that were the case, why Tyler should look almost as green as she had last night—just before she'd been ill.

Unless she was afraid the other woman might try to muscle in on her exclusive with him? Although even as that idea occurred to him he realized it didn't make much sense. Over the last seventeen years or so he had given hundreds of interviews; Tyler's interview, he had already determined, was going to provide nothing new.

'Yes, I'm Tyler Wood,' she finally answered the other woman. 'But I'm afraid we're in rather a hurry, so if you'll excuse us...?'

'But I just wanted to say—'

'I'm sorry, but we really do have to go now.' Tyler linked her arm with Zak's before turning them both determinedly in the other direction. Which was no easy thing, Zak acknowledged wryly, when he probably weighed almost a hundred pounds more than she did, and was also over a foot taller! A determined Tyler was obviously a force to be reckoned with!

Well, not this time. He was still angry with her over the photographer lurking outside the restaurant, and had no intention of going anywhere else with her this evening. Besides, there was still the puzzle of where he had seen the tall blonde before. Because, wherever it was, he had a feeling he didn't particularly like her.

And from the slight trembling he could detect in Tyler as she linked her arm with his, he didn't think she liked the other woman, either. Curiouser and curiouser.

'Aren't you being just a little rude, Tyler?' he murmured as she marched the two of them away from the restaurant—and the unidentified blonde.

Tyler shot him a warning glance, even as she kept on walking. 'I happen to think she was the one who was being rude,' she snapped. 'We were obviously in the middle of a conversation when she interrupted.' She suddenly looked as if she would have liked to bite off her own tongue for reminding him of that conversation.

As if he needed any reminding!

It wasn't as if he really cared who the other woman was—his only interest was in Tyler's reaction to her. And that was of no real importance when compared to the incident with the photographer.

He came to an abrupt halt. 'Forget it, Tyler. We aren't going anywhere.'

She blinked up at him in the illumination of the overhead street lamp. 'But you said—Calum McQuire—'

'I know what I said. But that was before.'

'Before what?' She glanced in the direction of the blonde, the other woman giving a rueful shrug before entering the restaurant.

'Before the photographer,' Zak reminded her grimly.

Tyler swallowed hard as she looked up at him. 'I told you I had nothing at all to do with that—'

'No?' he mocked. Who the hell else could have set that tender little scene up? 'Well, I guess we'll find out the truth of that tomorrow morning, won't we?'

He couldn't remember the last time he'd been so angry. Quite a lot of it was directed towards himself, Zak had to admit. He had been thrown slightly off balance by Tyler from the moment he'd met her.

She moistened gloss-covered lips. 'Tomorrow morning?' she repeated warily.

'Yes—if a photograph of the two of us appears in your scurrilous rag tomorrow morning, you can consider our deal null and void!'

It was what he wanted, anyway, to have this woman completely out of his hair, to call his life his own again, not to have to guard everything he did and every word he said, to wake up tomorrow morning and know that he never had to see Tyler Wood ever again.

Wasn't it?

CHAPTER SEVEN

TYLER blinked up at Zak, horrified at the thought of him terminating their interview.

She had to find Perry!

Now. If not sooner. Before he got anywhere near Bill Graham with the photograph of her and Zak, and the whole thing was taken out of her hands.

Not that it would stop her from personally throttling Perry when she caught up with him!

What did he think he was doing, taking photographs of her and Zak together? *They* weren't the story, and, from Zak's reaction to the photograph, he obviously didn't think they were, either. Much as a part of Tyler might wish it were otherwise...

She couldn't help but feel slightly relieved that something had diverted Zak's attention from the woman who had just approached her outside the restaurant; if Zak had realized who she was then he wouldn't wait for tomorrow morning, he would terminate their interview right now!

'I'm certain the photo won't be in *The Daily Informer* tomorrow,' Tyler assured him firmly.

He shrugged those broad shoulders. 'Let's wait and see, shall we?'

'And you really don't intend taking me to the party with you?' She frowned her disappointment; not because she wouldn't get to meet Calum McQuire after all, but because, despite the interruptions, she had actually been enjoying her evening out with Zak.

'I really don't,' he confirmed with a shake of his head. 'In fact, I suggest you take advantage of that cab—' he pointed back to the vehicle the blonde had just got out of '—and take yourself home.'

Tyler looked at him searchingly, realizing from his expression that he was completely serious. But as for his suggestion about her taking the cab—forget it! She had a few pounds with her, no mobile, unfortunately— it wouldn't fit into her small evening bag—and she wasn't about to use what little money she did have on a cab.

Even if she was wearing a Vera Wang dress!

Besides, she couldn't go straight home...

She drew in a deep breath. 'I think I'll walk, thanks. Where, and at what time, shall we meet up tomorrow?'

Zak's mouth twisted humourlessly. 'Pretty confident, aren't you?'

In a word—no! But she wasn't about to let Zak see that. 'I told you,' she reiterated. 'I had nothing to do with the taking of that photograph.' Even if she had a pretty good idea who did!

'And as I said, we'll see. If you don't intend taking the cab, then I will.' And without another word he got inside the idling cab, leaning forward to give the driver the address, before sitting back in the seat, not sparing Tyler so much as another glance as the cab moved out into the busy flow of evening traffic.

Tyler exhaled deeply, her shoulders slumping dejectedly now that she was alone. She was going to kill Perry when she caught up with him! After she had told him exactly what she thought of him, of course!

Her mood certainly hadn't improved an hour later when she finally limped into the newspaper office. The tube had been crowded, her red evening dress and high-heeled shoes earning her more than a little attention, mainly from leering males. Other women had given her pitying glances at being forced to travel on the tube in such a beautiful outfit.

But the walk from the tube station had to have been the worst of all, the high-heeled red shoes not meant for long walks on hard pavements, blisters forming on her heels, and her ankles aching.

'What the hell happened to you?' Bill Graham frowned as he looked up from his computer screen.

Tyler gave him a scowl for his trouble. 'Have you seen Perry?'

'This evening?' Bill shook his head. 'I thought he was supposed to be with you.'

'So did I,' she muttered, wondering where Perry could have gone after leaving the restaurant so hurriedly if he hadn't come here, after all. Home? Her apartment to wait for her? It looked as if she would have to try both places.

At least he didn't seem to have rushed straight over here with his photograph. That was something, but it in no way lessened Tyler's anger towards him. He had totally blown her evening out with Zak, and ruined her chances of a meeting with Calum McQuire. Although she had to admit it was the former that really bothered her...

'Where are you going now?' Bill could have added, Dressed like that? but didn't after a brief glance at her face dared him to do so.

Tyler grimaced. 'Home, I guess.' If only to change out of these clothes before continuing her search for Perry.

'Here, get yourself a taxi.' Bill reached into his

pocket and took a twenty-pound note from his pocket, throwing it across the desk towards her. 'It wouldn't look too good if one of our reporters got picked up by the police on suspicion of prostitution!' he explained at Tyler's obvious surprise at this kind gesture. 'Don't worry, I'll simply claim the twenty on expenses,' he dismissed before going back to his computer screen.

Tyler glowered across the desk at him. She should have known he wasn't just being nice—Bill Graham was never nice!

But to imply she looked like a prostitute!

Did she really look like a hooker in this dress? She looked down at herself in concern. It *was* quite a revealing dress, with its low neckline and ribbon shoulder straps, the style definitely figure-hugging. Even so, she hadn't thought she—

'You look great, Tyler,' Bill growled exasperatedly as he glanced up and saw her still standing there. 'Just get out of here, okay; some of us have work to do.' He pushed the twenty-pound note further across the desk before once again becoming engrossed in his computer screen.

Tyler picked up the money and left—before he changed his mind and decided to take the twenty pounds back!

But she didn't go straight home, instead directing the cab to take her to Perry's apartment. First she would deal with Perry, now that she knew he hadn't gone running straight to the paper with his photograph, and then she might be able to give some time to thinking about that chance encounter earlier with the woman outside the restaurant.

She had recognized the other woman, of course she had. The two of them might only have met the once, and then only briefly, but Tyler wasn't likely to forget Jane Morrow—the woman who had first given her the lead on the Jinx Nixon story.

Obviously Jinx's ex-editor hadn't forgotten Tyler, either. Not surprising really, in view of the fact that the other woman had lost her job through talking to Tyler!

But Tyler hadn't seen the other woman from that day to this. She hadn't particularly wanted to, either. She had little or no respect for Jane Morrow's work ethic once she had betrayed Jinx Nixon's confidence, and for no other reason, it appeared, than because she had had a huge unrequited crush on Nik Prince and was furiously jealous that Nik had only been interested in Jinx.

Luckily Zak hadn't been able to immediately place Jane Morrow, although Tyler wouldn't count on it remaining that way. He'd remember where he'd seen her sooner or later, and no doubt he would have plenty to say on the subject if he should ever recall who the other woman was!

He'd probably immediately jump to the conclusion that the two women were collaborating again on a story about Jinx Prince—or even, heaven forbid, Nik Prince. Tyler shuddered—it was well known that the Prince family were close. Zak would certainly go off the deep end if he thought that was the reason for Jane Morrow's appearance tonight. When the truth was, Tyler didn't have a clue what the other woman wanted!

Being around Zak, Tyler decided, was like balancing on a tightrope—one false move and she was likely to fall off!

It didn't help at all that suspicions were starting to

creep in that her high-school crush on Zak, far from fading away, was threatening to turn into an emotion more real and lasting now that Tyler had met the man himself. She didn't dare name that emotion. Even to herself. Privately. It was *far* too dangerous...

'What are you smiling about so happily?' Zak snapped after opening his suite door to Tyler's knock the next morning. He immediately wished he hadn't snapped at all as her smile faded to be replaced with a look of uncertainty.

But he was in a foul mood. Annoyed by what had happened the night before—especially after such a pleasant dinner together. Irritated at having to go to Calum's party alone, leaving him a target for all the unattached females there. And there had been plenty of them—all stunningly beautiful, all ready for a little fun. None of them making any secret of the fact that it was him they would like to have that fun with.

Unfortunately, without exception, each one of them, however witty or pretty, had left him cold.

Because all he'd been able to think about all night was Tyler. Of how she had teased and charmed him as they'd eaten dinner together. Of how absolutely stunning she had looked in that red dress. Of how he had been anticipating arriving at Calum's with Tyler on his arm. Of how she had set him up outside the restaurant...

But even that wasn't the worst of it—he'd been looking forward to the time after the party when he took her home, when he had intended kissing her senseless. Yes, much as he hated to admit it, it appeared he had committed that sin of all sins for an actor, and allowed himself to become attracted to a reporter!

He came back to an awareness that Tyler was still eyeing him in utter, adorable confusion.

'Is there some reason why I shouldn't be smiling?' she asked warily, dressed in black combats today, with a white figure-hugging tee shirt.

A tee shirt that outlined the perfection of her pert breasts—and which also showed Zak that again she wasn't wearing a bra beneath it!

Great, Zak moaned inwardly—now he was *lusting* after a reporter, too!

Those dark brown eyes looked troubled by his continued silence. 'But there was no photograph in *The Daily Informer*...'

'No, it would appear that you got to your boyfriend in time to stop that.' Zak's scorn was biting.

The colour in her cheeks deepened at his continued reference to Perry as her boyfriend, whether with embarrassment or anger, Zak couldn't be sure.

Tyler drew in a deep breath. 'I can assure you that Perry had no intention of publishing any photographs of you without first obtaining your permission. Admittedly, he was—a little overenthusiastic, last night, but—'

'Is that what you choose to call it?'

'Yes,' she maintained stubbornly. 'But when I saw him last night he assured me—'

'What? What did he *assure you*, Tyler?' Zak taunted. 'That he never intended taking that photograph to your editor? That he was just collecting material for this *exclusive* you keep talking about?' He could feel the anger building inside him, knew that his eyes were now as hard as sapphires, his expression

grim. He couldn't have stopped the words that tum-
bled out of his mouth next if he had tried.

'And did he assure you of this before or after he
took you to bed?' Zak ground out furiously.

Tyler blanched—in pain? 'I—he—you have no
right to say such things to me!' she finally managed
to gasp, those unfettered breasts quickly rising and
falling beneath her tee shirt in her agitation.

Zak remained hardened to the appeal in those deep,
deep brown eyes. 'No?' he challenged. *'No?'* he repeated, almost shouting now, reaching out to grasp her
arm and pull her inside his hotel suite before shutting
the door to give them some privacy. 'I think that
this…' he picked up a newspaper and thrust it in front
of her nose '…gives me the right to say to you exactly
what I damn well please!'

Tyler blinked up at him dazedly for several seconds
before reaching out with shaking hands to take the
newspaper from him, turning away as she scanned the
page in front of her.

Zak thrust his hands into his denims pockets in an
effort to stop himself from reaching out and shaking
her.

Oh, not because of what she was reading, although
he had memorized every word.

And speaking of love, it would appear that Zak
Prince, that prince of Princes, has a new mystery
lady in his life. The two, seen together at the fashionable O'Malley's last night, couldn't seem to take
their eyes off each other, and are said to be very
close indeed. Could The Prince be thinking of mat-
rimony this time…?

The article in the gossip column was garbage. Utter and complete garbage, even down to that stupid nickname the press had labelled him with a couple of years ago. But it wasn't what was written there that made him so angry. No, that was entirely due to Tyler. He had realized last night that he liked her, really liked her. The way she looked. Her quirky sense of humour. Her openness. Her *openness*! Hah, that was a joke!

Her face was still very pale when she turned back to him. 'But I— This isn't the paper I write for.'

'No, it isn't, is it? Which means that you kept to your promise that our photograph wouldn't appear in *The Daily Informer* this morning. You kept to the *spirit* of that promise,' he amended grimly, 'but that didn't mean that you couldn't chat to a rival gossip columnist, did it?'

Her eyes widened incredulously. 'You can't seriously think that I had anything to do with this article!'

'I'm trying not to think at all, Tyler,' he rasped harshly. 'In fact, I've been trying not to think since the daily newspapers were delivered outside my door at seven-thirty this morning!' The volume of his voice rose again, proof—if he needed it!—of just how furious he was.

But he didn't need proof. Just as he hadn't needed his brother Rik telephoning him from France at nine o'clock this morning, curious to know who the 'mystery lady' was! Apparently, the information that the story had appeared in the papers had hit the internet, which was where Rik had found it.

Not that he had given his younger brother the satisfaction of telling him anything about Tyler—least of all that she was a reporter. But having laboured through Tyler's paper from cover to cover, only to discover that there was no damning photograph, he hadn't exactly been thrilled when Rik had drawn his attention to the gossip in a rival newspaper!

'You were up at seven-thirty this morning?' was all Tyler seemed able to come back with.

He had been up at seven-thirty this morning for the simple reason he hadn't yet been to bed!

Calum's parties, although very infrequent, were always entertaining. Calum was that rare thing in the acting profession: completely his own man. This exclusive with Tyler, forced on Zak against his will, was enough to show him he wasn't that fortunate! But Calum was a man who did his own thing, having as many friends out of the acting profession as he had in it, and the mix of the two groups was always enjoyable.

Except Zak had been in a bad mood when he'd got there, completely unsociable for the first hour or so as he'd consumed several glasses of champagne. But eventually the friendly atmosphere had got to him, and he had relaxed enough to enjoy a lengthy conversation with one of the teachers from Calum's old school. Much to the chagrin of the beautiful women who had fluttered on the edge of his awareness!

It had been late—or early!—when he'd got back to the hotel at three-thirty, but he hadn't been able to sleep, had listened to music instead while he'd drunk all of the pot of coffee brought up to him by Room Service.

He had been waiting for the delivery of the daily newspapers, he had realized as he'd jumped up as soon as he'd heard them land on the carpet outside his suite. When the photo hadn't appeared in them, he had finally begun to relax, dozing off to sleep on the sofa when he'd found he couldn't even be bothered to undress and get into bed.

Only to be woken by the ringing of the telephone and a curious Rik's voice in his ear...

Zak knew Tyler had tricked him. He had only said their deal would become null and void if their photograph should appear in *The Daily Informer*. And it hadn't, had it? In fact, the photograph hadn't appeared anywhere. But the gossip about the two of them being seen out together was just as damning as far as he was concerned!

'Yes, I was up at seven-thirty this morning, Tyler,' he ground out between clenched teeth before finally taking his hands out of his pockets.

Not because he intended strangling her.

Oh, no, he had decided some time ago that that would be letting her off the hook far too easily.

No, he determined as he reached out to grasp Tyler's shoulders, if the gossip columnist had been informed—and it didn't take two guesses to know who by!—that he and Tyler were an *item*, then that was exactly what they would be. Why should he be subject to gossip based on absolutely no foundation?

'Zak...?' Tyler sounded innocently bewildered.

Deceptively innocent—as Tyler herself was!

And he had fallen for it. He had believed himself to be a man of the world, that he had seen it all, that he had become cynical even—because he knew every trick and ploy a woman cared to make to attract his attention. But Tyler had slipped under his guard, had fooled him into thinking she was exactly what she claimed to be—a reporter who just wanted to do an exclusive on him, one of those 'nice' articles that were so popular in expensively glossy magazines.

That might still be her intention. He didn't know—and, quite frankly, he didn't care, either. But what he did know was that Tyler wasn't above promoting herself by publicly linking herself with him. No matter how she had to accomplish it.

Some time early this morning, as he had sat fuming over the gossip column, wondering what to do next, he had decided that if that was what Tyler wanted then she could have it.

For a price!

CHAPTER EIGHT

ZAK was going to kiss her!

Tyler realized that only seconds before his head lowered and his mouth claimed hers.

She had dreamt of this—she had lied last night when she had claimed Zak had never featured in her dreams!—since she was fifteen years old. But in those fantasies it had never been like this. No, never like this!

Zak was angry, furiously so if their brief conversation was anything to go by. And that anger was his prime emotion as his mouth literally ravaged hers, the steely strength of his arms moulding her soft curves firmly against his much harder ones.

His fury and contempt for her was palpable, dictating his actions as his mouth demanded a response from hers, demanded and received it, despite the fact that Tyler was mentally screaming a silent 'no'!

This was just too much on top of what had already happened to her the last twenty-four hours: first that awkward meeting with Gerald in the restaurant, then Perry's stupidity in taking that unsolicited photograph, followed by Zak's response to it, and then meeting Jane Morrow. All of which had been followed by the most tremendous row with Perry when she finally had tracked him down at his apartment.

Oh, he had been all apologies, claiming that he hadn't meant to press the button on his camera at all, that the photograph had happened as a result of his shocked realization that she and Zak were about to kiss each other.

An excuse Tyler had listened to with scepticism. Only to have that emotion turn to guilt when Perry had then claimed he loved her, that he had been in love with her from the moment they had first met!

She had thought *that* was the final straw, until the gossip column this morning had quickly taken over that role—but this punishing kiss, here and now, was so much worse than anything that had happened before it.

Tears began to fall hotly down her cheeks.

Zak seemed to become instantly aware of this and raised his head sharply to look down at her with narrowed blue eyes. He held her out at arm's length as soon as he realized exactly how distressed she was.

'I thought this was what you wanted,' he growled. 'An affair with Zak Prince that you could write about in that rag you work for!'

To her mortification, Tyler was crying in earnest now, deep sobs that racked the slenderness of her body, no matter how hard she tried to control them.

No, this most certainly wasn't what she wanted! A return of the attraction she felt towards him would have been nice, a flirtation, possibly even something deeper if she were very lucky, but not—not this!

She drew in a deep breath. 'I had nothing to do with what's written in that gossip column.' She gave the discarded newspaper a disgusted glance. 'I don't know the person who wrote it. I don't want to know the person who wrote it.' Although a part of her was starting to wonder if she didn't know who was responsible for giving the information to the gossip columnist.

There was really only one person it could be—Jane

Morrow. And she had every reason to feel resentful towards Tyler, as well as wishing for vengeance on any member of the Prince family. Including Zak Prince.

But Tyler knew she couldn't tell Zak of her suspicions without bringing the other woman's name into the conversation, something she really didn't want to do if Zak hadn't realized himself yet who the woman outside the restaurant last night had been. And he obviously hadn't, otherwise that would have been something else he could challenge her with this morning.

'That's it, Zak,' she told him steadily. 'That's all I have to say on that subject.' She raised her chin, deep brown eyes clashing with accusing blue ones.

Only he looked perplexed now, frowning down at her for several long minutes, until a reluctant smile began to curve his lips. '"That's all?"' he teased.

Her brows rose in mute challenge. 'That's all,' she confirmed firmly. 'Believe me, or don't believe me, I've really got to the stage where I don't particularly give a—'

'No, don't spoil it, Tyler,' he protested. 'Do you want me to apologize?' He quirked one of his own dark blond eyebrows.

She blinked, then eyed him suspiciously, not sure what he would be apologizing for: kissing her so uncaringly, or for his accusations about her in the first place.

'That's really up to you, isn't it?' she said guardedly, her lips actually feeling a little swollen from the force of his kiss.

'Okay.' He nodded. 'I apologize. Unreservedly.'

That was a great help—she still had no idea what he was apologizing for! Why couldn't he just—?

She flinched back as Zak raised his hand towards her, that hand coming to an abrupt halt as he saw her involuntary movement. He scowled in sudden realization.

But what did he expect? He had just physically overpowered her. In fact, if she had any sense at all she would have walked out of here after proclaiming her innocence!

Zak moved his hand again, slowly this time, cradling her cheek, his thumb moving to gently touch the swell of her lips. 'I hurt you,' he said huskily.

Her tender lips were nothing compared to the hurt she felt inside at his complete lack of faith in her, professionally as well as personally. She tried to brush aside the fact that she was after as sensational an exposé on him as possible—*he* didn't know that! Just as he didn't know that she wouldn't jeopardize her chances of getting that story for a minor bit of tittle-tattle about the two of them that basically amounted to nothing more than embarrassment. For them both.

So he had been seen out with a 'mystery lady' who just happened to be her—so what? It was still no more than idle gossip. Irritating idle gossip, admittedly, but without the name of that mystery lady it was really pretty useless.

Although she, for one, was very relieved that there was no name—if anyone back home had read it and made the connection between the name Tyler Wood and her *real* name of Tyler Harwood, which she'd changed on arrival in England because of her well-known family, then she would really have been in trouble!

Zak looked pained, his thumb still moving soothingly across her lips. 'I really do apologize, Tyler. No matter what the provocation was, that's no excuse for my behaviour just now.'

'No matter what the provocation was?' she echoed. Did he still not believe her claim of innocence?

His mouth twisted wryly. 'No matter what I may have *thought* the provocation was,' he corrected ruefully.

'Better.' She nodded, much preferring him in this repentant mood to the formidable stranger who had met her at the door such a short time ago.

She had actually considered telephoning before coming over here, but had finally decided if she did that then she would just be giving him the opportunity to deny seeing her. She wished now that she had called first; at least that way she would have been forewarned about the gossip column—and Zak's feelings about it!

Although she didn't have any complaints about his behaviour at the moment...

The caress of his thumb against her lips was extremely sensual, so much so that her knees were starting to feel weak, heat building inside her. She was completely aware of how close he was standing to her, of the tangy elusiveness of his aftershave.

Tyler swallowed hard, her gaze locked with Zak's. 'Perhaps...' she stopped to clear her throat as her voice sounded huskily soft '...perhaps you could kiss it better?'

Zak's eyes widened slightly. 'Kiss it better?'

'Hmm.' She nodded, not a hundred per cent sure she knew what she was doing—but doing it anyway!

Minutes ago this man had been a cold, punishing stranger, but even then Tyler had known that wasn't the real Zak Prince. He had been angry, probably justifiably so after what had happened the previous evening and this morning, but once she had made a stand he seemed to have accepted her word that she was in no way to blame for that photograph or the gossip column.

She knew she was playing with fire, but as she had already burnt so many boats by coming to England in the first place, what was one more…?

He arched blond brows. 'You're sure about this, Tyler? I was angry before, now I'm just incredibly aroused,' he admitted gruffly.

She was well aware of that, had noted the way his eyes had darkened from sky- to cobalt-blue as his gaze rested on her mouth, the slight flush against his cheek-bones. Besides, he was standing so close to her now it would have been impossible for her not to feel the way his thighs had hardened against hers. With desire. A desire she echoed.

She moistened dry lips, her tongue accidentally stroking the sensitive swell at the base of his thumb, fire leaping in his gaze as he felt that hot, wet caress against his skin.

Tyler raised expectant eyes, still not sure if she quite knew what she was doing, or quite where it might end, but longing to feel Zak's lips against hers again, this time without anger.

One thing she did know seconds later—she was lost the moment Zak's mouth touched hers!

Her arms reached up over the broad width of his shoulders to wind themselves around his neck. She moved involuntarily against him, wanting to be closer still as his mouth worked passionate magic on her lips.

His hands felt hot on her back, as though they could burn through the material of her tee shirt. Then they slipped underneath her top, and she could feel them firm and caressing against the skin of her back, totally aware of wherever he touched her. Tyler gasped breathlessly as one of those hands moved around the front to cup her bared breast. The thumb that seconds ago had stroked her spine now moved skilfully, erotically over her hardened nipple, sending wave after wave of fiery warmth coursing through to deep down inside her.

It felt so good to have Zak touch her in this way, she thought, almost mindless with desire as she pressed herself deeper into his arms. She was on fire, trembling, shaking, the throbbing ache between her thighs becoming almost unbearable. Almost…!

It felt too good for her to ever want Zak to stop. She had never experienced anything like this before, so overwhelmingly aroused she could feel and see nothing else but Zak.

Oh, God!

As the pleasure continued to wash through her with every beat of her pulse nothing else existed. Nothing else mattered except Zak and the incredible passion that only he could make her feel. Her entire body felt as if it were melting, the force of their combined desire taking her to heights she had never known before.

She wanted this never to stop, wanted nothing else, needed nothing else as Zak's lips and tongue now moved moistly over her bared breasts, capturing first one pouting nipple and then the other, drawing it deeply into the heat of his mouth—

'What the hell…?' Zak responded dazedly to the sharp rap he had heard on the suite door. He was completely aroused from the feel of Tyler's caressing hands on his chest and back beneath his unbuttoned shirt. And he was totally absorbed in the perfection of her swollen, creamy breasts with their gorgeous crushed-raspberry nipples.

'There's someone at the door.' He groaned as he reluctantly released her and pulled down her top to avoid the temptation to just carry on where they'd left off—despite the person now standing outside the door! 'I'd ignore it, but if it's Housekeeping again come to clean my room then they'll just let themselves in,' he explained at the look of confusion on Tyler's face.

It had always been convenient for him to live in a hotel whenever he visited England, but just recently he had begun to realize that it also had its drawbacks—lack of privacy being the main one!

He strode over to the door and opened it impatiently. 'Yes?' he barked irritably at the man standing outside in the corridor—obviously not Housekeeping!

'David Miller, Mr Prince,' the other man introduced himself briskly at the same time as he thrust out his hand in greeting.

Having absolutely no idea who the younger man was, Zak shook that hand warily.

David Miller smiled brightly. 'I'm following up on the column in the— Mr Prince!' he protested as Zak moved to close the door on him. 'Is that the "mystery lady"?' The man—another reporter!—glanced quickly past Zak into the suite and saw Tyler. 'Hey, don't I know you—?'

The slamming of the door cut off the rest of what the reporter had been about to say, and Zak scowled darkly as he turned to look at a red-faced Tyler.

This was getting ridiculous, Zak decided. He was used to the media being overly interested in his private life, but over the years he had managed to reach an unspoken agreement with most of them: they would basically leave him alone and then when there was something for them to report he would let them know about it. All that mutual goodwill seemed to have evaporated since Tyler Wood had exploded into his life!

God, Tyler! She had felt fantastic in his arms just now, her skin as soft as velvet to the touch, every inch of her body completely responsive to his. As his was to hers...

He had never felt such overwhelming desire for a woman before. Oh, there had been plenty of women in his life, probably too many, he admitted honestly to himself. But never anyone quite like Tyler before.

He wanted her. Desired her. Needed her. But at the same time he had sensed an inexperience about her, as if she were surprised by her own response to him, surprised, but at the same time eager for the feelings to continue. And that, in turn, made Zak feel protective towards her.

Which was probably the most ridiculous thing about this whole situation. Tyler was twenty-six years old, beautiful, feisty, and fighting for her place in a male-dominated career; it was highly unlikely that she was sexually inexperienced!

Or maybe it was just that she had the ability to make a man feel that she was...?

Zak thrust his hands into his denims pockets as he frowned across at her. 'Miller seemed to think that he knew you; does he?' he asked, still not completely sure he bought her claim of innocence concerning that gossip column.

Could this second reporter turning up at his hotel suite out of the blue, conveniently while Tyler was here too, be perhaps too much of a coincidence?

The same thought seemed to have occurred to Tyler as she suddenly looked worried. 'Not personally, no,' she answered slowly. 'But we were briefly introduced at a press conference a few months ago.'

Zak arched blond brows sceptically. 'By whom?'

She shook her head, her gaze no longer quite meeting his as she replied, 'I don't remember.'

Was it just that she didn't remember, or could it be that she actually knew David Miller rather better than she was willing to admit to Zak, of all people?

Whatever, the other man's timely interruption had certainly put a dampener on the passionate interlude in each other's arms—and wherever that had been about to lead!

That could have been the whole intention, of course, Zak allowed wryly. But no—how could they have arranged that when even Zak hadn't known it would happen? It looked as if he was becoming completely paranoid where Tyler was concerned, although, after the last few days of such 'coincidences', he couldn't exactly be blamed for that!

'Whatever,' he dismissed. 'Do you think it likely that Miller will remember where he knows you from?' In his opinion—and at the moment that could be slightly biased, he allowed—no man was ever likely to forget having met Tyler.

'I don't know that, either—I'm not a mind-reader, Zak!' she objected as he gave a derisive snort.

At the moment, that was probably just as well, he conceded ruefully. A few minutes ago he had been thinking quite seriously about taking her to bed for several hours—days!—and just forgetting who and what she was, of forgetting that the rest of the world existed, in fact.

Way to go, Zak, he mentally mocked himself. Very mature and responsible.

Except that mature and responsible were the last two things he felt around Tyler. Slightly wrong-footed and dazed by lust probably best described how he felt whenever he was with her. Which wasn't a good thing to be around any sort of reporter!

The main problem was, he still wasn't sure what sort of reporter Tyler was...

'How do you intend going about finding out where he knows you from?' he prompted curiously.

Her eyes widened. 'Me?'

'Yes, you. You appear to know who he is, so you probably know which newspaper he works for too.'

'Well...yes,' she admitted irritably. 'But if I start asking questions it's only going to add to his speculation—'

'Not my problem.' Zak shrugged.

'Well, it certainly isn't mine!' she protested.

'No?' he mused. 'Then you aren't at all bothered at the thought of having your name and face plastered all over some newspaper in connection with mine— you are bothered?' he jeered as her face distinctly paled, her expression panicked before she managed to replace it with one of uninterest.

That same panic he had seen in her earlier when he had first shown her the gossip column...

Tyler Wood was hiding something, he realized shrewdly. Although quite what that could be, he had no idea... Yet.

'My presence in your hotel suite is easily explained as business,' she protested. 'I'll simply give David a call and explain the real situation to him.'

Zak gave a humourless grin. Humourless because,

although she might see her presence here as just 'business', he had ceased to think of her in that way long ago. Probably from the moment he'd first looked into her chocolate-brown eyes.

'That's certainly one way of dealing with it,' he allowed. 'And the sooner the better, don't you think…?' he added pointedly.

Tyler blinked, and then frowned as his meaning became clear. 'You want me to go *now*?'

'Yes, I want you to go now.'

Because if she didn't go soon he was going to forget everything else and start kissing her again—and this time he'd remember to put the 'Do Not Disturb' sign on the door first! And that was a very bad idea. No, he badly needed Tyler to leave. Right now. If not sooner!

Then, hopefully, by the time he saw Tyler again, he would have this desire to kiss her and never stop back under control again. Hopefully!

No woman had ever had this effect on him before, where he felt a need to kiss and shake her at one and the same time. And until he knew more about Tyler—something he intended rectifying the moment she had gone!—it would probably be better for everyone concerned if he did neither of those things.

Tyler, it seemed, was something of a 'mystery lady' after all, if not quite in the way that the gossip columnist had implied. She knew someone of Gerald Knight's fashion-designer status, quite well if their friendly greeting the previous evening was anything to go by. Which seemed to imply there was more to it than her having just written an article on the man.

Also, her relationship with her photographer, Perry Morgan, was rumoured to be a lot more than platonic.

And yet no one he had so far spoken to seemed to know anything about Tyler before she had arrived in England six months ago, intent on making a name for herself as a reporter.

Which posed the questions: where had Tyler been for the first twenty-five and a half years of her life? Where did she come from? Who were her friends? Her family? The main question Zak wanted an answer to—and he already knew he wouldn't get that from Tyler herself—was why none of the people she had met and befriended in England knew anything about her other than the little she had told them.

What was Tyler hiding?

Because she was definitely hiding something...

CHAPTER NINE

'AND so I just wanted to ask you, if by some remote chance Zak Prince should contact you, not to tell him anything you know about my private life.' Tyler looked pleadingly across the table at Gerald Knight as the two of them had lunch together.

At her request. Because there had been something in Zak's manner when they had parted this morning, a spark of suspicion, that made Tyler want to close all the doors behind her before he had a chance to go through them and start asking questions about her.

Somewhere, somehow, during the last twenty-four hours, Zak had neatly turned the tables on her, so that *she* was now the one evading answering questions about herself!

Gerald arched mischievous dark brows. 'By "private life" I'm presuming you mean I'm not to discuss Rufus or the fact that you're calling yourself Tyler Wood now and not Tyler Harwood?'

'Yes, that's exactly what I mean,' she said, at the same time only just resisting the urge to look around them to see if anyone might be listening to their conversation. Was she being paranoid, or what? 'It's bad enough that Zak thinks I'm some flaky female rookie—if he finds out who I really am then he'll never take me seriously as a reporter!'

He laughed softly. 'I would love to be a fly on the wall if Rufus and Zak were ever to meet!'

'They never will,' Tyler vowed, shuddering just at the thought.

'Oh, I wouldn't be too sure about that, Tyler darling,' Gerald mused, wearing a cream suit today, with a yellow shirt and cream tie. 'From where I was sitting last night, and that column in the newspaper this morning, Zak Prince seems to be pretty interested in you.'

She felt the warmth colour her cheeks. 'You're wrong,' she insisted flatly. 'I'm interviewing him, and that's all. Now promise me, Gerald. Please!'

He gave in gracefully, saying, 'You know I never could resist your gorgeous brown eyes.'

One down, Tyler accepted gratefully, only David Miller to go—although she knew it would be a lot more difficult to get any information out of him—such as who had set him onto her and Zak. Tyler hadn't exactly been truthful this morning when she had told Zak she didn't remember who had introduced her to David Miller, but she was sure the person who had introduced them didn't have anything to do with all this. Could Jane Morrow have gone to David Miller then, in an attempt to cause yet more trouble for the Prince family? Tyler hoped finding Miller would answer these questions.

However, in the meantime, dealing with these problems certainly gave her something else to think about other than Zak's lovemaking. She really, really didn't want to go there. At the moment, she couldn't handle where those thoughts might take her...

And she didn't think about it. Not once all afternoon. Until she returned to her desk at the newspaper and glanced across the busy room to see Zak comfortably ensconced in Bill Graham's private office!

Her eyes went wide and her legs trembled. She

reached out to grab the edge of her desk, her face paling, as through the window of the office she actually saw Bill laugh—Bill never laughed!—at something Zak had just said to him.

But that wasn't the only unusual thing about Zak being in Bill's office; the door was firmly closed, and Bill's office door was never closed. He liked to keep his ears as well as his eyes open when it came to his staff.

A staff that might as well not have been there as far as Tyler was concerned, her whole attention focused on Bill's office and what might be happening in there right now.

What on earth was Zak doing here? Men of his calibre and fame never usually stepped into any newspaper office willingly. The media followed him, not the other way round!

'He's even better looking in the flesh, isn't he?' Callie Rhodes, part of the fashion team, winked at Tyler suggestively as she walked past her desk.

The colour flooded back into Tyler's cheeks as she remembered exactly how much of that flesh she had seen on Tuesday morning as well as today. How much of that flesh she had actually touched!

'Lucky old you,' Kelly Adams, a fellow reporter, sighed longingly as she also strolled past, her gaze fixed on Zak.

Oh, yes, lucky old her!

Had Zak come to complain to Bill about her method of reporting?

She hadn't exactly been too successful in interviewing him—her complete awareness of Zak, her response to him, seemed to render her completely incompetent as a journalist every time she was anywhere near him!

Zak was standing up now. The two men were smiling at each other as they shook hands, before Bill moved to open the office door and escorted Zak out into the main office.

Zak walked straight towards her, that smile still curving those beautifully sculptured lips.

Tyler stood rooted to the spot, a look of absolute horror on her face, her eyes still wide with the shock that Zak was here in the first place.

'Hi, Tyler,' he greeted lightly as he neared her desk, his expression totally unreadable.

'Hi, Zak,' she managed to return through barely moving lips.

'Bye, Tyler.' He raised a hand in parting as he continued to walk straight past her desk towards the door.

'Bye, Za— Hey, just a minute!' she burst out of her stupor to protest, moving to hurry after him as he headed towards the lifts. But not before she had noticed Callie, Kelly, and every other female in the vicinity gazing at him with sickening doe eyes.

But then, if Zak had bestowed that smile of warm, lazy charm on her, as he just had on them, she might have joined them!

'Zak!' she called out to stop him from actually getting into the lift, lengthening her stride as she joined him in the corridor. 'What are you doing here?' she demanded to know as he looked down at her.

He shrugged broad shoulders beneath the black tee shirt he wore, fitted denims resting low on his hips. 'I don't mean to sound rude, Tyler,' he drawled, 'but do you really think that is any of your business?'

Angry colour burned her cheeks at this put-down. 'Bill Graham is *my* boss,' she objected.

'And is there some law that says I can't come in and talk to him?'

Her hands clenched into fists as she glared up at him. 'No law, it's just—Bill is my boss,' she repeated ineffectually. But if Zak had some sort of complaint to make about her—and he probably had lots!—she would much rather he had discussed them with her rather than with Bill Graham. 'Does this mean my exclusive with you is at an end?' If she was off the story, then she was out of a job, too... 'Did you ask Bill to take me off the story?' she enlarged with impatience as Zak continued to look puzzled.

'Why would you think that?' he asked.

Any number of reasons! She had a snap-happy photographer following her around. It was because Zak had been seen out to dinner with her the previous evening that his name had appeared in a gossip column this morning. And probably worst of all—and neither of them had referred to it for some time—she had been sick all over the carpet in his hotel room before spending the night recovering in his bed!

She shrugged. 'Things haven't exactly been running smoothly the last couple of days—'

'Running smoothly?' Zak exclaimed incredulously. 'Tyler, it's been nothing but one disaster after another since the moment we met!'

Tyler blanched at this blunt statement, but she couldn't leave it there. She barely glanced at the lift as it arrived at their floor, the doors opening automatically. 'That hasn't all been my fault,' she defended herself weakly—knowing that most of the disasters he was referring to had indeed been her fault. Even if she had done nothing personally to cause them!

'Well, it certainly hasn't been mine,' Zak argued as

he stepped into the waiting lift. 'Are you free for dinner tonight, Tyler?' he added unexpectedly.

'Oh! I—er—yes,' she accepted finally, totally taken aback by the invitation; their conversation so far certainly hadn't indicated that he wanted to spend another minute in her company, let alone an entire evening!

'Fine.' He turned and pressed the button for the ground floor. 'And if you happen to have another Vera Wang in your wardrobe, I should save it to wear on Saturday evening,' he advised her enigmatically.

Tyler gave him a startled look. Saturday night? What was happening on Saturday night?

'I'll see you at my hotel at around eight this evening, okay?' he added as the lift doors closed—with him inside, and Tyler still standing in the corridor wondering at exactly what point she had completely lost control of the conversation.

No, that was wrong, she instantly chided herself— she had never *had* control of the conversation in the first place! In fact, she had no idea what Zak had been talking about half the time.

Saturday night was just one more indication of that. What was happening on Saturday night that Zak wanted her to wear something as exclusive as a Vera Wang dress to? she wondered as she wandered back to her desk. She did have another one, as it happened, in fact she had—

'He is one gorgeous man, Tyler,' Kelly gushed effusively as she paused on her way out of the office.

'Yes,' Tyler acknowledged vaguely, although an inner part of her—an unreasonable, jealous part!—resented Kelly's obvious attraction to Zak. He certainly was gorgeous, and there was no doubting that his kisses melted her all the way down to her toes, but she didn't like hearing another woman commenting on his good looks. Which was pretty ridiculous if she thought about it.

For one thing, the way Zak looked was part of his acting success; she very much doubted he would be quite as successful if he looked like Godzilla's uncle! And for another thing, she simply had no right to resent anything where Zak was concerned. No matter how much she might wish it were otherwise.

'Do you know who this mystery lady is in his life?' Kelly probed.

Tyler had always liked the other woman, both personally and as part of the reporting team, but at that moment she dearly wanted to tell Kelly to mind her own darned business!

'I don't think there is one.' She managed a small rueful smile at the other woman. 'Our competitor must have just been short of gossip this morning.' She gave a dismissive shrug, hoping the other woman wouldn't continue the subject.

'Oh.' Kelly looked disappointed. And then she brightened. 'Oh, well, perhaps there's still hope for the rest of us, after all. See you later, Tyler,' she added brightly before hurrying back to her own office on the next floor.

Leaving Tyler feeling decidedly disgruntled. With three people.

With Kelly for her obvious drooling over the man Tyler was more and more convinced she was falling genuinely in love with; it was positively the last thing she wanted, but she was very afraid it was already a fact.

With Zak himself for the totally bewildering conversation they'd just had.

And, finally, with Bill Graham, because he had been chatting away with the younger man, even laughing with him at one stage, and she still had no idea what they could possibly have been talking about! Knowing Bill as she did, he probably wouldn't tell her either, if she were to ask. Which was—

Saturday night!

Tyler dropped weakly onto her chair behind her desk as the full significance of that day finally hit her with the force of a sledgehammer.

It was the reason Zak was still in England after attending his brother's wedding last weekend. The reason he had been able to give her the time this week to do the interview with him at all.

Saturday night was the English première of Zak's latest film *Gunslinger*!

And from the little he had just said to her, he was expecting her to accompany him to it...

There was absolutely *no way* she was going to appear in such a public way with him, to the interest of reporters and photographers alike—*worldwide* reporters and photographers...!

'So although it's a very—gracious thought on your part, I'm afraid that I have other plans for Saturday night, which means I will have to decline your invitation,' Tyler concluded breathlessly as she sat next to Zak in the cab they'd hailed after leaving his hotel shortly after eight o'clock that evening.

Zak listened, with complete indifference, to her refusal to attend the première with him on Saturday evening. Because, no matter what she might think to the contrary, she would be going with him. Either that, or she would have to tell him the real reason she didn't want her own name or photograph appearing in the newspapers on Sunday morning.

Zak was more convinced than ever that this was the real motive behind her refusal. He had been trying all day to find out more about his so-called 'mystery lady', but it was as he had thought; either people—like David Miller—didn't know anything about Tyler before she'd come to England, or others that did—like Bill Graham and Gerald Knight—simply weren't talking. In fact, Gerald Knight hadn't spoken to him at all, because he had been 'unavailable' all day.

So he had come up with a plan that was sure to elicit some sort of response from Tyler, and in so doing perhaps give him an insight as to what—or whom—she was running away from in the States.

Her halting claim to having other plans for Saturday night was certainly a start!

He gave a falsely rueful shrug. 'Then I guess you'll have to change or postpone those plans.'

'I'm afraid I can't do that,' she protested stiffly.

'That's a pity,' Zak said unsympathetically. 'Bill Graham seemed to like the idea when I discussed it with him earlier today.'

Tyler stared at him incredulously. '*That's* what you were discussing with him earlier?'

He arched mocking brows. 'He didn't tell you?' Although he wasn't surprised the other man had left it up to him to discuss this with Tyler; he had the distinct feeling that Bill Graham was one of those people, although he liked to pretend otherwise, who knew a lot more about Tyler Wood than he was willing to divulge, to Zak or anyone else. Possibly even to Tyler herself...

'No, he didn't tell me,' she snapped angrily. 'Unless

it escaped your notice, Bill Graham isn't a man who likes to make life easy for the people who work for him!'

'I did notice, actually,' Zak drawled. 'Nevertheless, he totally approves of your attending the première with me. In fact, I think he likes the kudos of having one of his reporters in the limelight,' he added provocatively.

Because Bill Graham probably guessed—knew...?— that Tyler felt totally the opposite!

Tyler drew in a deep breath, obviously about to launch into yet another refusal to attend the première, when her attention was caught and held by the fact that the cab had turned into a private driveway. Zak gave her a brief smile before getting out of the cab and punching the code into the security device that automatically opened the huge iron gates.

She looked slightly confused as Zak got back in beside her, the cab now driving up to the front of a tall, imposing Victorian house. 'Where are we?' she finally asked as Zak came round to open the door for her to get out of the cab.

Zak answered as he turned back from paying the driver, 'My sister Stazy also saw that gossipy piece about the two of us in the newspaper this morning.' Probably aided and abetted by Rik, he inwardly acknowledged grimly. 'She's invited the two of us for dinner this evening,' he added, at the same time taking a light hold of Tyler's arm.

A move she totally resisted, pulling her arm out of his grasp to step back. 'You have *got* to be kidding!' she cried incredulously, looking absolutely horrified at the thought of meeting yet another member of the Prince family.

But it was a statement that Zak wholeheartedly sympathized with where his sister was concerned; Stazy might be the youngest in their family of four siblings, but as the only female, and happily married herself, she had since become quite formidable in her matchmaking efforts for her three older brothers.

From their brief telephone conversation this morning, Zak had the distinct impression Stazy wanted to know more about this 'mystery lady' in his life, hence the invitation to dinner this evening. But it wasn't an experience Zak intended going through alone!

'Believe me, you don't kid around with someone like Stazy,' he informed Tyler as he rang the doorbell. 'She may not be very old, but she's become decidedly bossy since she married a year ago.' And he had to admit to feeling a certain curiosity about what his sister would make of Tyler.

A Tyler who still looked absolutely horrified at the prospect of having dinner with a member of his family!

'If it makes you feel any better, her husband Jordan will be there too. Jordan Hunter, of the Hunter Brothers hotel chain,' he added, attempting to be reassuring, but only increasing Tyler's trepidation if her now-apprehensive expression was anything to go by.

What she actually looked was incredibly beautiful, the black fitted, knee-length dress suiting her slenderness, her make-up light, and for once her hair not in that spiky style that reminded him of an angry porcupine, but falling softly onto her forehead and curling back behind delicate ears.

He received a glare for his effort at trying to help her feel more relaxed, Tyler giving a disgusted snort before turning as the front door was opened by his sister; Stazy, as a hugely successful interior designer, was wealthy in her own right, and Jordan was a millionaire several times over, but Stazy resisted having any live-in staff in the house, preferring to make a home for her family herself.

Zak stood slightly back as the two women looked at each other, knowing by the way Stazy's eyes widened that she, at least, was pleasantly surprised by Tyler. He wondered briefly what the women he was usually involved with were like, because Stazy had never approved of any of them!

Not that he was altogether sure she approved of Tyler either as Stazy's smile faded to be replaced by a perplexed frown as she continued to look at Zak's companion. Zak could sympathize with the emotion— it was how Tyler made him feel most of the time, too!

Tyler was the one to break the silence that was beginning to stretch out so long it was seriously in danger of becoming awkward. 'Hi, I'm Tyler Wood,' she greeted brightly. 'I believe there's been some sort of misunderstanding concerning my being seen with Zak a couple of times.' She gave a—forced?—laugh. 'The "mystery lady" in Zak's life is actually just a reporter doing an exclusive interview with him. Your brother Nik actually arranged it,' she added pointedly.

So much had happened this week since he had first met Tyler that Zak had to admit that he had almost forgotten that little fact!

But obviously Stazy hadn't, her frown fading slightly. 'Of course,' she replied. 'Why didn't you just explain to me earlier, Zak? I'm sure Tyler can't really want to have dinner with your family,' she chided as the three of them went inside the house.

And miss out on all the fun of spending another

evening in Tyler's company? Besides, when Stazy had invited them for dinner, he really had forgotten the real reason Tyler had come into his life when he'd accepted for the two of them! It just showed how complicated his life had become the last few days. Probably because his two prime emotions during that time had been anger and desire—both of them directed at the tiny, beautiful woman at his side.

'We were meeting up this evening anyway. Besides, I didn't want to miss out on a free dinner!' he teased, to direct the attention away from his error.

Stazy laughed. 'Go through and join Jordan, you clown. I'll just take Tyler upstairs so that she can freshen up before we eat.'

Tyler already looked fresh enough to him. In fact, he was finding it hard to keep his eyes—and everything else!—off her. But who was he, a mere man, to question the need to reapply lipstick or whatever?

'Fine.' He nodded, turning off into the sitting-room, where he intended asking his brother-in-law for a whisky and soda. A large one!

CHAPTER TEN

'OKAY, Miss Harwood,' Stazy Hunter said abruptly as soon as she had closed the bathroom door on the two women. 'I believe you have about five minutes to tell me exactly why you're masquerading as a reporter named Tyler Wood!'

Tyler stared in horror at her hostess. Stazy stared right back at her, that implacable Prince will Tyler had already run up against several times with both Nik and Zak clearly in evidence, her grey eyes hard and un-blinking, the previously smiling mouth set in a deter-mined line.

Tyler had thought things were going so well—she had got this far in England without anybody discov-ering her real identity. Maybe she could still save the situation...

'And it had better be good,' Stazy Hunter continued harshly. 'Good enough to convince me not to march straight down those stairs and tell my brother exactly who you really are!'

Tyler swallowed hard, a little shaken by the other woman's challenge. 'So you know who I am?'

'Well, of course I know who you are,' the younger woman snapped. 'And so would Zak if he had ever read any of the society magazines over in America! You're that New York socialite who's practically the arbiter of fashion, make-up and hair-dos over there.'

Tyler gave a rueful smile. 'Hardly Zak's scene, is it?'

'No,' his sister conceded dryly. 'But it's certainly *yours*,' she accused. 'I'm still waiting, Tyler, and the minutes are ticking away.'

She raised an auburn eyebrow in pointed enquiry.

Tyler's thoughts were racing madly. What could she tell her? What could she possibly say, when Stazy obviously knew exactly who she was, that would convince this woman that her own intentions were completely honest where Zak was concerned?

Especially as they *weren't* completely honest, a little voice in her head reminded her reprovingly.

Okay, so maybe they weren't, but her interview with Zak had nothing to do with the reason she was over here working as a reporter under an assumed name, did it?

Of course it didn't. She hadn't even known she would so much as meet Zak Prince when she had made that initial decision six months ago.

So maybe if she just told Stazy the truth about why she had come here six months ago and her reasons for keeping it private—especially from Zak—it would be enough to avert disaster.

Maybe it was the relief of finally being able to talk freely about herself, or perhaps it was just that Stazy looked so set on not moving until she knew what was going on, but once Tyler started explaining, the whole story just came tumbling out.

Stazy didn't show any reaction as Tyler began talking. She just listened, giving Tyler no indication as to whether or not the other woman believed a word she was saying.

'After the most awful row with my parents, in particular my father because I'd rejected his choice of husband for me, I just packed a bag, booked myself a ticket for London, Heathrow, and here I am,' Tyler explained. 'I changed my name because it's so well known both here and in the States, and I didn't want to get a job on the back of that or, even more likely, have job applications refused because I was perceived as an empty-headed bimbo who was only worried about her hair and nails! As for not telling Zak who I am, I figured that if he knew he'd just stop taking me seriously as a reporter—not that he takes me that seriously professionally, anyway,' she finished up ruefully.

Stazy finally moved, shaking her head. 'I wonder why it is,' she mused, 'that dominating men just don't see themselves as being that way.'

Tyler made no reply, the statement not really requiring one; those men just didn't see themselves that way.

But did that comment mean that Stazy believed her?

Stazy sighed. 'Believe it or not, I did something very similar myself eighteen months ago, including changing my name.' She grimaced. 'Three older brothers, who always think they know what's best for their little sister, is just three too many, let me tell you!' She chuckled softly. 'And Zak really has no idea who you are?'

'None,' Tyler confirmed—although she was sure Zak had some suspicions that she wasn't quite what she appeared to be!

'Hmm.' The younger woman considered. 'Well, at this point in time, I'm not sure that he needs to know, either.'

'Do you mean it?' Tyler pounced hopefully. 'Are you really not going to tell him?' It seemed a little too good to be true!

'At this point in time,' Stazy reiterated. 'But if that situation changes, if I think for one moment that Zak is going to be hurt by not knowing—I'll tell him.'

'He won't be hurt,' Tyler hastened to assure the other woman, able to think of no circumstances where her real identity might affect Zak. And she wasn't being dishonest in her claim; the exposé she was supposed to write on Zak might not go down too well, but her real name shouldn't make any difference to that.

'Are you sure about that?' Stazy gave her a searching look. 'This is the first time Zak has ever brought anyone to dinner here.'

'But only because you made a point of inviting me,' Tyler protested.

'And you think this is the first time I've ever issued such an invitation to any of the women Zak has been involved with?' Stazy asked with a smile.

Tyler didn't want to hear about any other woman Zak had been involved with! 'He isn't involved with me,' she assured the other woman, even as she could feel herself blushing once again. Those twin flags of colour, for one reason or another—usually to do with Zak!—seemed to be becoming practically permanent fixtures in her normally pale cheeks. 'I told you, I'm just spending a week interviewing him.'

Stazy still looked far from convinced. 'You have to know that, as far as I'm concerned, Zak always comes first.'

'I wouldn't expect anything else,' Tyler acknowledged, seeing this as further evidence of how close the Prince family really were. 'But by not telling him who I am, I'm not hurting Zak, I assure you.' At this moment she was willing to promise the other woman anything if it prevented Stazy from telling Zak who she was!

Stazy gave a glance at the slender gold watch on her wrist. 'We've been far longer than five minutes,' she announced. 'The men are going to wonder where we've got to.'

Not noticeably so, Tyler thought wryly as the two handsome men, one tall and dark, the other tall and honey-blond, broke off their laughing conversation to introduce Tyler and Jordan to each other.

To her surprise, after that rather shaky start, Tyler found herself enjoying the evening, the conversation flowing easily. The Hunters were obviously a very happily married couple, and Zak's relationship with both of them was pleasantly easygoing too. In fact, despite her earlier apprehension, it turned out to be the most relaxed and enjoyable evening Tyler had spent since coming to England.

'Thank you for including me this evening,' she told Zak huskily on the drive back. 'Stazy and Jordan are nice.'

Zak eyed her teasingly. 'And being my sister, you didn't think Stazy was going to be?'

'No, of course I didn't think that,' Tyler fired up immediately. 'I just—you're winding me up again, aren't you?'

'Only a little,' he assured her softly. 'What were you two women talking about upstairs for so long when we arrived?' he asked innocently.

Too innocently? It certainly seemed so to Tyler. But Stazy had appeared genuine in her promise not to tell Zak about who she was unless absolutely necessary. And certainly nothing had happened yet this evening for that situation to have changed.

'Just fashion and things,' she said evasively. 'Totally boring as far as you men are concerned.'

'Aren't you being a little sexist there?' Zak taunted. 'I'm sure Gerald Knight, for instance, would be very interested.'

'Gerald?' she echoed a little too sharply; after her worries earlier in the day, it seemed a little coincidental that Gerald should be introduced into their conversation.

Zak nodded. 'Ladies' fashions would obviously be of interest to him.'

'Only because it's what he does,' she retorted. 'I meant that, as a general rule, ladies' fashions—'

'—and things,' Zak put in dryly.

'—are of little interest to most men.'

'You're right.' He nodded. 'No interest whatsoever.'

Then what had the last few minutes' conversation been about? He was probably still trying to wind her up. He really was—

'Perhaps you would like to tell the driver your address,' Zak prompted.

Tyler gave him a startled look in the dimly lit interior of the cab. 'My address?'

'Mmm. It occurs to me that, although we've had dinner together twice now, I've never actually collected or taken you back home at the end of the evening. It's time I rectified that.'

She didn't want Zak to take her home! She didn't want Zak to know where she lived. In fact—

'Just what exactly are you hiding, Tyler?' He seemed to guess some of her thoughts, his gaze narrowed now. 'A husband and six kids? Or could it be—' his voice had hardened slightly '—that you share your apartment with someone, after all?'

'Of course I don't—'

'Perry Morgan, for example,' Zak added as if she hadn't spoken, a scowl darkening his eyes now.

'I've already told you I don't share my apartment with Perry,' she reminded him indignantly. 'I don't share my apartment with anyone!'

Zak was quick to take advantage. 'Then there's no problem with my taking you home, is there?'

Of course there was a problem. A big problem. Her apartment was her own space, her very own space, the first she had ever had; if Zak ever went there she would never be able to go home again without remembering him there. And feeling about him as she did, that would be unbearable.

Besides, there was also another factor involved here; earlier this evening Zak had completely overridden her objections to going to his film première with him on Saturday. No matter what he thought to the contrary, she still had no intention of going with him—despite what Bill Graham might or might not have to say about that!—but if Zak actually knew where she lived, he might prove harder to evade than she wished. In fact, hiding out in her apartment seemed to be the only answer to that particular problem!

She was going to fob him off with yet another excuse; Zak knew it before she even spoke.

He had been pleasantly surprised this evening by the easy way Tyler got on with Stazy and Jordan; his sister wasn't known for giving the current woman in any of her brothers' lives an easy time of it!

But maybe the difference here had been the fact that

Tyler had gone to great lengths to let Stazy know she wasn't, in fact, the current woman in his life!

It had deeply irritated him at the time. What exactly constituted being 'in someone's life'? Spending time together? He and Tyler seemed to have done a lot of that the last few days. Kissing each other? Well, he and Tyler seemed to have done that several times too.

In fact, to all intents and purposes, whether Tyler wanted it or not, she was very much in his life!

But she so obviously didn't want to be his current woman. Which was why he knew she was going to make some feeble excuse about not taking her home, let alone actually inviting him up to her apartment!

'The thing is, Zak—' she spoke quietly '—I just don't want to take you there.'

Not feeble at all! Just the straight, unvarnished truth. He had come to admire that about her, in spite of himself.

He gave a rueful laugh. 'Try to spare my feelings, why don't you?'

'I just think it's time we put things back on a businesslike footing,' she explained.

He was very much past businesslike where this woman was concerned. Hell, he had passed that point the moment he had laid Tyler in his bed three nights ago.

She had been ill, and had looked it, but, at the same time, while she'd been asleep that slightly aggressive expression she habitually wore hadn't been in evidence, giving her a delicately appealing look. And he was as vulnerable to that as any other man would be.

Not that he had seen her defences down again in quite that way since; in fact she was usually prickly enough to frighten off most men's interest in her.

Maybe it was arrogance on his part, but he had just never thought of himself as 'most men'...

Admit it, Zak, he inwardly chided himself, you're far too interested in a woman who's running in the opposite direction so fast you have difficulty keeping up with her, let alone getting one step ahead of her! Maybe that was half the novelty to him; he was usually the one doing the running! Whatever the reason, he was so interested in Tyler he could almost believe he was falling in love with her, if that idea weren't so ludicrous. A famous actor, in love with a tabloid reporter...he could see the headlines now!

'Put things back on a businesslike footing?' He repeated her words now. 'Exactly how have we got along with that so far? What do you actually have to write for your article at the moment?' he enlarged as she looked puzzled.

Was it his imagination, or did her cheeks become slightly flushed at his reminder that they'd done more kissing than interviewing to date? Bill Graham had been quite convincing earlier today that there really was an article. In fact he had confirmed to Zak that he had it in mind for the Sunday supplement magazine.

And yet Zak was sure he detected a slight embarrassment in Tyler every time he mentioned the article. Which meant that Bill Graham was either a better actor than he would have given the other man credit for, or Tyler was just embarrassed at her lack of interviewing skills so far.

No doubt it was a little difficult to ask questions when the subject of the interview was kissing you! As he wanted to kiss her again right now...

Once again Tyler looked beautiful this evening, the

plain black dress deepening the brown of her eyes and giving a peachy glow to her bare neck and face. She had also proved to be a very funny dining companion as she'd regaled them with stories earlier about some of the vocabulary mistakes she had made when she had first come to England.

Stazy, he could tell, had liked the other woman very much, and Jordan had been enchanted by her. In fact, if it weren't for the fact that Zak knew Jordan was totally and utterly in love with Stazy, he would have found his brother-in-law's teasingly indulgent manner towards Tyler meritous of a punch on the nose!

He had been jealous.

Even though he had never experienced the emotion before, Zak knew and recognized the feeling for what it was. That destructive, character-changing green-eyed monster he had heard so much about but had never experienced until now.

It was one of the reasons he so badly needed to kiss Tyler again. Away from curious eyes and interruptions, so that the two of them might explore their emotions— Who was he kidding? He wanted to be alone with Tyler so that he could make love to her until she was senseless. Until they were both senseless!

'In retrospect, we haven't been businesslike at all,' she answered his question huskily. 'Which is why I suggest that tomorrow we spend the day together so that you can read through a list of questions I've compiled.'

Spending the day together sounded okay to him; him having to read through a list of questions less so. 'Isn't my just giving answers to a load of pre-written questions going to come across as just a little stilted in your article?' As well as being excruciatingly laborious on his part.

The truth was, he just didn't want Tyler to see him struggling to read the damned questions!

This was his real—his only—secret from the public. He had been labelled a troublemaking rebel during his high-school days, the wild one of the Prince brothers. But what no one had realized for quite some considerable time was that the reason he was always bored and getting into trouble was because most of the classes just went completely over his head, and that textbooks were just a bewildering jumble of letters to him.

Dyslexia. He was an adult before it had actually been diagnosed—along with his IQ of one hundred and sixty!—but once it had been, his reading difficulty had ceased to be much of a problem. With two older brothers, and a very young sister, all of them eager to read things to him and help him memorize his scripts, the issues that had dogged his school life had just faded into the background. In fact, he rarely gave them a thought nowadays.

Dyslexic. What a name to give to someone with reading difficulties—he could barely say it, let alone read it, and it was a sure fact that he couldn't spell it! He was pretty sure that most dyslexics felt the same way. They were people challenged by the formation of a sequence of letters into a readable word, and putting a label like dyslexia on it only served to confuse the people afflicted with it.

And it was something Zak didn't want Tyler, or indeed any other reporter, writing about!

Other successful actors who had been open about their dyslexia had already proved that dyslexics weren't idiots—far from it, they were just letter challenged. But Zak had decided long ago that he didn't need, or want, anything written about him to begin with 'dyslexic this' or 'dyslexic that'; it was a learning disability, and he wanted to just leave it at that.

Tyler's face was still flushed at his previous comment about her article possibly sounding stilted. 'I like to think I have the ability as a reporter to write the article in such a way that it doesn't just appear like a question-and-answer thing.'

'Let's hope so,' he said. 'Coming in for a nightcap?' he invited as the cab came to a halt outside his hotel.

'I won't, if you don't mind,' she refused abruptly, obviously still smarting from what she saw as his implied criticism of her reporting skills.

Zak sat back from paying the driver. 'And if I do mind?' he asked huskily.

She met his gaze unblinkingly. 'I'm still not coming in.'

He couldn't help it, he laughed, once again wanting to kiss her as well as shake her. He could never remember feeling that way about any woman before. 'You're one stubborn woman, Tyler Wood.'

Because of the unhelpfulness of those people who knew her, whether deliberate or otherwise, he still knew little more about her this evening than he had this morning. But that didn't mean he wasn't still determined to find out more. By fair means or foul.

Knowing Tyler as he did, he had a feeling it was going to have to be foul!

She gave a rueful smile. 'It takes one to know one!'

He raised surprised brows. 'You think *I'm* stubborn?'

She gave a derisive smile. 'I think you are many things—and stubborn is just one of them.'

Zak laughed again. 'Maybe you should come inside and tell me some of the other things I am?'

'That *I* think you are,' Tyler corrected dryly. 'And the answer is still no.'

He shrugged. 'You can't blame a guy for trying!'

In fact, he wanted to do more than try with Tyler. Much more. That was the problem. And until he knew more about her, where she came from, who, if anyone, was waiting for her back in the States, he was wary of even attempting to try and take their relationship further.

That was what the rational side of his brain told him, anyway.

The other part, the part that wanted to pick her up in his arms and carry her upstairs to his suite—pretty much as he had on their first evening together, except this time he wouldn't give Tyler any brandy!—said to hell with caution and just go for it!

'I don't blame you for anything, Zak.' She sighed wearily. 'I've just had enough for one night, okay?'

No, it wasn't okay, not really, but from her tone of voice, that slightly defensive air, he knew he didn't have any other choice.

'Okay,' he accepted before leaning forward and kissing her lightly on the lips. 'Thank you for a lovely evening, Tyler; I enjoyed it.' It was the truth, after all; he had enjoyed the evening. He had just hoped to be able to kiss her—no, more than just kiss her—at the end of it.

She had looked slightly disconcerted after he'd kissed her, but now she laughed. 'Goodnight, Zak.'

''Night, Tyler. Same time tomorrow morning?' he added as he got out of the cab.

'Same time tomorrow,' she echoed huskily.

By fair means or foul, he reiterated as he stood on the pavement and watched the cab drive away...

CHAPTER ELEVEN

'OH, NO, not again!' Tyler groaned as she looked down at the newspaper Bill Graham had just slapped down on the desktop in front of her, his expression grim.

She had come into the office early this morning—did Bill never go home?—intending to check on her e-mails and other messages, deal with any other paperwork, before taking the tube over to Zak's hotel.

This photograph, on the front page, no less, in yet another rival newspaper, of her and Zak getting into a cab, Stazy and Jordan Hunter standing in the doorway of their home as they waved goodbye at the end of the previous evening, told her that wasn't going to happen.

'How did they even get this?' She groaned, her hand moving instinctively to cover the photograph, as if by doing so she could block it out. Except she knew that she couldn't, that hundreds, thousands of copies of this exact same photograph were appearing on the front page of this newspaper as it was distributed all over the country. The world, perhaps?

Her face paled even more as she realized the consequences of that happening. She really didn't want her father butting into her life right now!

She took her hand off the photograph, staring down at it intently now. She was just about to get into the cab, her face turned slightly away from the camera, but was it enough so that the casual observer wouldn't recognize it as being her? She was thinner than she had been six months ago, and her hair was shorter too, so maybe, just maybe—

'Actually, Tyler,' Bill cut in on her racing thoughts, his tone sarcastic, 'I'm more interested in why this paper have this photograph and we don't! Where the hell was your boyfriend Morgan when all this was happening?' He glared down at her.

'He *isn't* my boyfriend,' she responded automatically, still staring down at the photograph. 'You know, the downward angle of this photograph means the photographer must have been standing on the wall or something,' she said slowly.

'Who the hell cares where they were standing?' Bill exploded. 'He, or she, got the damned photograph and we didn't!'

That wasn't all he or she had got; the headline with the photograph screamed the caption, ZAK PRINCE TAKES HIS 'MYSTERY LADY' HOME TO MEET THE FAMILY! Zak was going to kill her. Slowly.

Except... This was all his fault. *He* had arranged that dinner last night with Stazy and Jordan. Maybe *she* would kill *him*. Slowly!

She grimaced. 'I doubt Stazy and Jordan Hunter will see it quite that way. Maybe they'll press charges for invasion of privacy,' she added with satisfaction.

'And a lot of good that will do them.' Bill snorted. 'Tyler, if you're having an affair with the man, then why—?'

'I am *not* having an affair with Zak Prince!' she cut in fiercely.

Bill raised his eyes heavenwards. 'Okay,' he sighed. 'If you're *involved* with Zak—'

'I'm not *involved* with him, either,' she insisted.

'Bill, you of all people know exactly why I'm spending time with Zak Prince.'

'And a lot of good it's doing me!' he snapped. 'From the looks of this photograph, you're too busy socializing with the man to have come up with anything on him of any interest!'

Anything sensational, Tyler knew he meant. Something, as she spent more time with Zak, she was becoming increasingly reluctant to do even if she did find out any deep, dark secrets about him!

A great reporter she was turning out to be! Maybe Rufus had been right after all—she really wasn't hard enough for the cut-throat career of journalism. Maybe she should just give up and— No, she mustn't even think that way. She *had* to succeed at this. She just *had* to. It was what she had said she would do when she had walked out on her life six months ago, and she had to do it!

'All I'm trying to say, Tyler…' Bill sighed his frustration with the situation '…is if you do get involved with the man then give us the heads up on it first, hmm? Remember where your loyalties lie, okay,' he added before going back to his office, the slamming of the door behind him enough to confirm his bad temper.

If Tyler had needed any confirmation. Which she didn't.

She looked down at the photograph again. Could anyone tell it was her? Really tell, unless—like Bill— they already knew she was spending time with Zak? Probably not, she decided critically. In fact, it could have been any one of hundreds, thousands, of tiny brunettes getting smilingly into the cab.

And yet, under any other circumstances, she would

have been proud to be photographed with Zak Prince, would have been ecstatic if she really were the 'mystery lady' in his life. If she were the woman in his life at all!

But this was different. This was deliberate stalking, and not just by one reporter or photographer, but a number of them. Which meant she had to take action immediately. If it was Jane Morrow behind this, then she had to somehow find her and stop this vendetta against the Prince family, as well as herself. Before someone really got hurt.

'Tyler!' A pleased voice broke into her reverie.

She looked up to see Perry entering the office, relieved to see the cheerful grin on his face. She had to admit to having avoided him since his declaration of love the other day, but there was nothing in his smiling face now to indicate the incident had ever happened. Which was fine with her. She liked Perry; in fact, he was the only real friend she had made in England, and she certainly didn't want to spend the rest of her time here avoiding him.

'Perry,' she returned warmly, at the same time turning the newspaper on her desk face downwards; she didn't want to start Perry off again on his dire warnings about Zak. She had already had enough of those this morning from Bill! 'I think Bill is looking for you,' she informed him.

Perry glanced across at their boss's office. 'Is that good or bad?' he asked as he sat on the side of her desk, as handsome as ever in casual tee shirt and denims.

Why couldn't she have fallen in love with nice, uncomplicated Perry? Why couldn't she have fallen in love with anyone except Zak Prince?

Because she hadn't, she accepted heavily. It was Zak that she loved, that she would probably always love.

She shrugged, standing up. 'I'm really not sure.' She avoided answering the question. 'And I'm afraid I have to get going now; I have an appointment this morning.'

'Zak Prince again?' Perry frowned.

'Just my luck, huh.' She deliberately made light of the subject.

'How about lunch later?' Perry stood up too, blue eyes intent.

She gave a regretful grimace. 'I'm really not sure, Perry. I'll call you, okay?' She smiled encouragingly. Although not too much so; she didn't want to give Perry the wrong impression. Again.

She was still a little stunned by Perry's proclaimed feelings for her. She didn't think she had given him any encouragement, but she couldn't be sure. Especially when Zak and Bill both seemed to assume that Perry was her boyfriend!

'Fine,' he said breezily, obviously determined to keep this conversation light and unpressured.

To her relief. They might never get back to that easygoing friendship they had once shared—at least, as far as she was concerned—but it would be nice if they could at least talk to each other without embarrassment.

'See you later, maybe,' she told him as she left.

The conversations with Bill and Perry had seriously cut in on her time, meaning she would have to go straight to Zak's hotel, rather than trying to find Jane Morrow first. But she would take the earliest opportunity to get to her—she had to stop this harassment before it got completely out of hand.

But she had other things on her mind now apart from Jane Morrow or Perry. Thanks to the photograph in that paper, she was absolutely dreading meeting up with Zak this morning. It would be just too much to hope that he hadn't seen that phograph. And even if he hadn't, she knew, in the circumstances, that she would have to tell him about it.

He had already seen it!

One look at his long-suffering expression as he opened the door to her knock, and Tyler knew there were no confessions or explanations necessary. Although she was a little taken aback by his first comment!

'I'm really sorry to be putting you through all this, Tyler.'

'I—you're sorry?' She blinked up at him; this was not the reaction she had been expecting from him.

'Yes,' Zak rasped. 'Someone, it appears, is playing games with us. And I don't like it.'

Tyler thought she knew exactly who that someone was, but she was still loath to bring Jane Morrow's name into the conversation. She had managed to make one brief call on her mobile on the journey over here, but Jane Morrow's last employer had refused to even talk about the woman. His secretary had been a little more forthcoming, commenting that she believed the other woman was now a literary agent.

Tyler hadn't yet had time to follow that lead up, but she would do so once she left Zak later today.

In the meantime, Zak's reaction to the photograph of the two of them was something of a surprise.

'Maybe someone just got lucky?' She shrugged as she walked into his suite.

'No, I don't think so,' Zak murmured as he closed the door behind her. 'It seems too—insistent, for that.'

'Insistent?' she repeated lightly—knowing exactly how insistent Jane Morrow could be! 'Because of the première on Saturday, maybe?' she suggested. 'After all, that's sure to increase the interest being shown in you by the press. And talking of Saturday,' she added determinedly, 'I hope you've found someone else to accompany you to the première?'

Zak shot her a mocking glance. 'Now why would I do a thing like that?'

Because there was this—thing, between them, that shouldn't be there. A sort of frisson that appeared whenever she was anywhere near him, which set all of her senses and nerve endings onto alert. It was there now, had sprung into action the moment she'd looked at him. No, even before she'd looked at him, the excitement singing in her veins having increased with every passing mile of the journey over here.

God, she loved this man. Loved everything about him. The way that his honey-blond hair fell endearingly over his brow, each of those handsomely chiselled features that so often contained such teasing mischief, the way he looked good wearing a faded tee shirt and scruffy denims that moulded to the hard contours of his waist and hips, even his bare feet sensual in their male perfection. And she wasn't even a person who particularly liked feet! But she loved Zak's feet, as she loved everything else about him...

She gave a wistful sigh before answering him. 'It really isn't my scene, Zak.'

Which was yet another lie on her part. Before

England, before she'd become simply Tyler Wood, she had attended numerous movie premières, as well as charity balls and fund-raising events for everything from underprivileged children to an endangered species of monkey in the African jungle.

In the States, she could have attended the première of *Gunslinger* with little reaction, except the usual prestigious mention of her having been there. As Tyler Harwood she would have been *expected* to be there!

What would Zak have made of her then? A vacuous social butterfly who picked and chose to put the weight of her name to whatever charitable fancy took her at the time.

Would he have even *liked* Tyler Harwood? Somehow she doubted that. Just as she knew he certainly wasn't going to like Tyler Wood once she had written her scandalous exposé on him!

What a depressing thought.

'Tyler?' Zak was looking at her searchingly now. 'Tyler, are you crying?'

She hadn't thought that she was. In fact, if anyone else had asked her that question she would have answered a scornful 'no'. But just Zak asking the question seemed to make it so, hot tears burning behind her lids before falling down her cheeks. Making it impossible for her to deny it!

'Damn it, you *are* crying!' Zak groaned even as he reached to take her into his arms, holding her closely against him, one hand cradling the back of her head, the other moving soothingly up and down her spine.

Oh, God…!

Those already alerted nerve endings and senses suddenly went berserk as the feel and smell of Zak bombarded them, her knees feeling weak and wobbly as she clung to the broad width of his shoulders.

'If you don't want to go to the première, then you don't have to!' Zak muttered, straightening slightly, both hands moving up to cradle either side of her tear-wet face as he kissed first one damp eye and then the other. 'I hate it when you cry,' he grated. 'Even if you do look more beautiful than ever,' he added huskily as he looked down at her.

Tyler gave a choked laugh. 'Then you're the first man I've ever known to find red eyes, soggy cheeks and a runny nose beautiful!'

'On you I do,' he assured her. 'Although I'm not sure I like the idea of other men having made you cry.' He frowned darkly.

'Just you, hmm?' she teased, very aware that at this moment the world had narrowed down to just the two of them, Tyler and Zak, Zak and Tyler, that anything else, her past, Zak's present, their lack of a future together, had faded completely into the background.

Zak shook his head. 'I don't want to make you cry, Tyler. Making you cry doesn't come anywhere near the list of things I would like to do to you!'

Her heart actually seemed to stop beating completely for a moment or two, her breathing catching in her throat as she stared up at him. The blue of his eyes was deeper than ever, her own image reflected back at her in the black depths of his dilated pupils.

She swallowed hard before drawing in a shaky breath. 'You have a list of things you'd like to do to me?'

'I have a list,' he confirmed softly. 'And last night's chaste kiss goodnight isn't anywhere on it!' he joked.

She had gone to bed dreaming about that kiss! Had

lain awake for hours, it seemed, hugging that kiss tightly to her.

Because she knew her time with Zak was limited? Because she knew that once she had found his Achilles heel, and written about it, that Zak would never want to see her again?

Yes, because of both of those things, she acknowledged heavily. Both of them, and at the same time neither of them. She could take, oh-so-briefly, the little Zak had intimated he was prepared to give, aware from what he had said just now that he was open to the suggestion of an affair between them. But when he learnt the truth about her, when *The Daily Informer* hit him right between the eyes with where that intimacy had taken him, he was only going to hate her all the more.

She didn't want that. Couldn't live with that.

'I have a list, too,' she told him brightly, stepping back from him to turn away from the sudden confusion she could read in his expression, to reach into the depths of one of the leg pockets of her combat trousers. 'Here it is.' She produced her notebook, turning it to the applicable page before handing it to him, at the same time hardening her heart to the disappointment she could now see clearly on his face.

She had made enough mistakes in her life already without adding a relationship with Zak to their number! It was far too late to stop herself from falling in love with him, but she couldn't further complicate that by entering into a full-scale relationship with him, a relationship he could later accuse her of using to her advantage.

Even if every instinct in her body cried out to be in his arms, in his bed, and damn the consequences!

Zak looked down at the notepad Tyler had handed him, taking longer than usual in his confusion to sort out the jumble of letters into some sort of readable order. But once he did, he realized this was the list of questions Tyler had intended asking him today in connection with the article she was writing.

How the hell had they moved from her being beautiful, and his having a list of things he wanted to do to her, to *this*!

'I know it probably looks a bit daunting,' Tyler continued in that bright, jaunty voice. 'But if we just go through them one at a time, I'm sure we can—'

'Tyler, don't talk to me as if I'm six years old!' he growled, closing the notepad with a firm snap before flinging it down onto the coffee-table. 'What the hell happened to the tears? A few minutes ago you were in my arms because you were upset, and now you're— well, now you're back to business!' And while she might be able to turn her emotions on and off at will, he certainly couldn't—his body was still hard from her close proximity. An arousal she must have been well aware of!

Was that the reason she had pulled back when she did? Was Tyler the one playing games now? Damn it, he was thirty-six years old—he didn't play that sort of game. With anyone.

She frowned. 'I think it's for the best, don't you?'

Whose best? His? He certainly didn't enjoy these hot and cold moods of Tyler's, having to draw back from the brink time and time again.

So it must be for Tyler herself. But why? She was attracted to him; he was experienced enough to be completely sure of that! So what was holding her back? Another man? She had told him she wasn't involved with Perry Morgan, that she lived alone, but that didn't mean there wasn't someone waiting for her back home in the States...

It was the only explanation that seemed to make any sense. And while he might applaud her will-power in resisting the attraction between the two of them, couldn't she see that the fact there was an attraction between them meant she couldn't be completely emotionally committed to this relationship back home?

'Tyler—'

'Zak, you may as well stop right there, because I am not going to have an affair with you!' she cut in forcefully as he would have made a step towards her, at the same time holding up one of her hands to ward him off.

He came to an abrupt halt, his eyes glowing with anger that she felt she had to hold him off at all. 'It's usually polite to wait until you're asked!' he snapped, not enjoying the way she flinched at his words, but at the same time needing to hurt her as she was hurting him.

Because he liked Tyler. Hell, he more than liked her! He had never felt this way before. Never wanted to kiss a woman, and yet at the same time protect her, in the way that he wanted to with Tyler.

He looked forward to seeing her every day, had woken up this morning with a smile on his lips because he had known that in a few hours he was going to see Tyler again.

He had spent most of yesterday trying to find out more about her—and not succeeding too well, he admitted—but now, today, he had realized that he didn't need to know any more about her than he already did, that it didn't matter any more, that just being near her was enough.

He was in love with Tyler!

And that emotion was completely alien to him. Totally. Oh, he'd had crushes on girls when he was in high school, had liked and enjoyed the company of several of the women he had been involved with over the years, but nothing he had felt for them was anything like what he now felt for Tyler. Just the anticipation of seeing her again was enough to make him feel good, being with her somehow making him complete.

That she didn't feel the same way about him was painfully obvious! Feeling as he did, he could never have pulled back from her in the way she had from him just now. Damn it, despite everything, he still wanted to take her in his arms and make love with her!

'I'm sorry.' Her gaze didn't quite meet his now. 'You're right, I shouldn't have just assumed—maybe I should just go now? I mean, I doubt you will want to continue with the interview today after—this,' she added awkwardly.

This? She called it 'this' in that way? He had just realized that he was in love for the first—and last?—time in his life, and she dismissed it as if what was happening between them was something rather unpleasant she would rather just forget!

Tyler didn't feel the same way that he did, he told himself again, feeling a sharp pain strike his heart. She couldn't, or they wouldn't even be having this soul-destroying conversation.

It was ironic really, if he thought about it. The Eternal Bachelor, Zak Prince. The Elusive Prince. The

Prince of Princes. All of the ridiculous names the media had labelled him with over the years! And when he did finally fall in love, when he no longer wanted to be elusive, or indeed a bachelor, the woman he was in love with didn't feel the same way about him!

It would even be funny—if it didn't hurt so much!

'You're right, I don't want to continue with the interview,' Zak bit out harshly, turning away; just looking at Tyler right now was too much.

Tyler looked uncomfortable now. 'Er—shall I come back tomorrow, then?'

Tomorrow? Would anything have changed by tomorrow? Would he no longer be in love with Tyler? Would she have suddenly discovered that she loved him, after all? None of those things was likely to happen, Zak chided himself bitterly—but especially the last one. Which was the only one that mattered.

'I'll call you,' he snapped. 'At the newspaper,' he added as he realized he didn't even have her mobile number. 'Later,' he rasped. Much, much later. Next century, maybe!

'Fine,' she accepted shakily. 'I—there's a few things I need to do today, anyway.'

What things? Zak wanted to know. And who, if anyone, was she doing them with?

This was unbearable!

Zak Prince, the man who never became seriously involved, was in love with a woman who refused to even tell him her private telephone number, let alone anything else about her life! She knew all there was to know about him, and he—

The phone rang. He had never thought he would be grateful for the interruption of the ringing of the telephone, and he scowled as he saw Tyler was just as relieved. 'Stay where you are,' he instructed grimly before picking up the receiver, his eyes widening as he easily recognized the voice on the other end of the line. 'Max, it's the middle of the night in LA!' he calculated after a brief glance at his wrist-watch.

'Still early,' his friend dismissed airily. 'Besides, you told me to call you if I came up with any answers for you on this Tyler Wood thing. Although I think I should warn you, old buddy, this isn't coming for free, I'm going to want some answers about her from you in return.'

'Fire away,' Zak invited, watching Tyler with narrowed eyes even as he listened to Max.

She had moved to look out of the window, giving every appearance of not listening to his end of the telephone conversation. Not that there was a lot to hear, Zak deliberately keeping his responses to Max to a simple yes or no.

Which wasn't to say he wasn't finding Max's conversation interesting. Because he was. *Very* interesting.

'I owe you one, Max,' he told the other man warmly when Max had finished talking. 'But later, okay?'

'The fair Tyler wouldn't happen to be there right now, would she?' Max guessed astutely.

'As a matter of fact, yes,' Zak confirmed. 'And it's brunette, not blonde.'

'Beautiful?'

'Oh, yes.'

'I'll leave you to it, then.' The other man chuckled before ringing off.

Zak put the receiver down slowly before looking across at Tyler as she turned to look at him, the silence stretching between them as his gaze narrowed.

'What?' she finally questioned, her chin raised defensively, her body tense.

'That was a friend of mine in LA,' Zak told her unnecessarily; she had to have been able to work that much out from his conversation. 'It appears that Tyler Wood never wrote an article on Gerald Knight in any publication in America.'

He watched with interest as she visibly paled.

'You've been lying to me, Tyler.'

CHAPTER TWELVE

TYLER stared at Zak, unable to speak, unable to think, it seemed. He— They— It—

'You've been checking up on me?' she finally managed to gasp.

She had suspected as much yesterday, but nothing had prepared her for this. So much for warning Gerald not to say anything!

With the release of her vocal cords, her thoughts began to race too. Zak had someone in America checking up on something she had told him. If he had gone to that extreme about a casual remark, what else had he done? That visit to Bill Graham yesterday—had that been checking up on her too, rather than discussing the première as Zak had claimed?

Dear God, what else had this Max in America managed to find out about her?

Zak's mouth twisted humourlessly. 'Don't go all pretend indignation on me, Tyler—'

'There's no pretence about it!' she said heatedly, an angry red haze blinding her to anything else but the fact that Zak had been making enquiries about a Tyler Wood back home.

How had Zak's friend got his information? Whom had he talked to in order to find out there was no article on Gerald Knight written by Tyler Wood? Because if he had talked to the wrong people—

She didn't even want to think about that! Besides, Rufus was in New York, not Los Angeles, and as such it was highly unlikely that he would get to hear about Max's enquiries. And even if he did, he might not connect her to the Tyler Wood they were talking about.

Keep telling yourself that, Tyler! Rufus, she knew from experience, had far-reaching tentacles in the media world, and it wasn't such a big step to take to get Tyler Wood from Tyler Harwood! She should have chosen a completely different pseudonym, but she'd stuck to something close to her real name because she'd known she'd forget to answer to it otherwise!

She glared at Zak. 'You had absolutely *no* right to pry into my personal life—'

'Your *professional* life, actually, Tyler,' he corrected her calmly. 'Something that, in the circumstances, I have a perfect right to ask about. And I'm still waiting for an answer,' he reminded her.

'And you'll continue to wait,' she spat. 'Because, after this, I have no intention of telling you anything. In fact, I think it might be better if we terminated this whole interview right now.'

She knew it would be suicide as far as her career at *The Daily Informer* was concerned; Bill Graham had left her in absolutely no doubts about that. But far better she get fired from the paper than Zak continued to probe into her background in this intrusive way. If she were no longer pursuing this exclusive with him, he would have no further reason to ask questions about her, here or in America.

The ironic thing was, if he just asked his sister Stazy the right questions, she could tell him everything about Tyler he might ever wish to know! Well, as much as Stazy was aware of, anyway.

'Running away, Tyler?' Zak jeered.

As far and as fast as her legs—and possibly a jet plane?—could carry her!

But where could she go? France? She only spoke a rudimentary French, certainly not enough to live and work in the country. Germany? Ditto. In fact, that applied to all the European countries. Canada, maybe? The same language, and yet still a separate country. Hmm, maybe that would be worth considering—

'Tyler?' Zak's voice brought her sharply out of her reverie, his narrowed gaze fixed shrewdly on her as if he had half guessed that running away might be closer to the truth—and a lot more permanent—than he had thought.

'You seem to have all the answers, Zak,' she hissed, eyes flashing. 'Work it out for yourself!' She was so angry with him that half of her just wanted to lash out at him. But the other half of her wanted to dissolve into tears again!

She had known Zak was trouble from the moment she had met him; what she hadn't realized was that he wouldn't be satisfied with just stealing her heart, he would completely knock her legs out from under her careerwise too. Bill Graham would have no other choice but to fire her for incompetence after she failed to get a story on Zak—and she wasn't sure she didn't deserve it!

She had come to England to prove herself, as a reporter and as a person, and so far she had completely blown the story of the decade by allowing Nik Prince to play on her emotions, and now she had compounded that mistake by falling in love with his brother. To add insult to injury, she also had another man, a man she thought of only as a friend, madly in love with her, which had made life decidedly complicated.

Maybe she really wasn't safe to be let out on her own!

Zak was shaking his head now. 'You have no reason to run away from me.'

'Oh, yes, I most certainly do. Why couldn't you just leave things alone, Zak?' Her voice, to her chagrin, broke emotionally this time, instantly betraying how distressed she was by his actions.

'What is it, Tyler?' He looked at her searchingly. 'Who are you running away from?'

She couldn't tell him—if there was still even the tiniest chance she could prove herself as a reporter, then she would. With or without Zak's input.

'Today? That would be you,' she snapped. 'But tomorrow it could be someone completely different.'

'I don't believe it—you aren't a woman who runs away. Towards something, maybe, but never away from it.'

It was what she had told herself when she had left New York six months ago, but maybe she had been wrong about that, too? Maybe she had been running away all this time?

The truth was, she could have found her own apartment in New York, could have found a job too—maybe not reporting, because Rufus really did have a finger in every media pie in New York. But she could have found a job of some sort, could still have proved her independence that way.

Couldn't she?

She just didn't know any more. Falling in love with Zak, having him talk to her in this way, having him believe she was fearless, had shaken her belief in what she was doing.

She swallowed hard. 'Zak, you don't know me. You

may think, with that call from your friend, that you know more about me now than you did last night. But you don't really know me,' she repeated flatly, not even sure she knew herself any more.

She needed to go somewhere, completely quiet and free from stress, and work out exactly what she was doing with her life.

'But, don't you see? I'm *trying* to know you!' Zak practically growled in frustration.

She gave a humourless smile. 'When you think that you do know me, give me a call, hmm? I'd like to know the answer to that one, too!'

'Tyler, is this reaction just because I had a call from a friend in LA?'

'Not really,' she sighed. 'But perhaps we should just forget doing the interview, and I'll do what I can to stop the invasion of your privacy that's been happening the last few days—'

'You *know* who it is?' He frowned as he glanced down at the photograph of the two of them in the newspaper.

'Yes, I think so. But don't worry, I'll deal with it.'

'You'll—!' Zak broke off exasperatedly. 'Tyler, just give me a name and I'll deal with it myself.'

She met his gaze unflinchingly. She still didn't want to bring Jane Morrow's name into any conversation with him. In typical protective Prince fashion, he was already up in arms about the mischief Jane Morrow had tried to cause between Nik and Jinx. If he thought Tyler was contacting her again, he'd probably assume Jinx's ex-editor was still intent on making mischief, and that Tyler was aiding and abetting her to get a good story!

'I don't think so.' She shook her head, turning away

so that he wouldn't see the tears gathering in her eyes—she had to get out of here before she shed any of those! 'If you'll excuse me, I think I should go now—'

'Just like that?' He grasped her arm and turned her back to face him. 'Tyler, what the hell is going on here? Three days ago you were desperate for this interview, and now you're just walking away? I don't get it.'

Desperate? Was that really how she had appeared to him on Monday morning? Yes, she probably had, she thought, feeling rather crushed.

Three days ago, before she'd come to know this man, she had been hungry for his story, determined to prove herself, no matter what the cost. Now she no longer knew what she wanted. Except she didn't want to do anything that would hurt Zak. And she didn't want anyone else to do anything to hurt him, either...

She gave a dismissive shrug. 'It isn't working out the way I expected.' And how! Despite her schoolgirl crush, falling in love with Zak had never been part of her plan.

'And just what did you expect?' Zak asked.

In all honesty? After the things she had read about him, the charmed life he led, the women he was involved with, she had thought Zak Prince would shatter all her girlhood illusions and turn out to be a pampered, arrogant man who revelled in being a movie star. What she had discovered was that she couldn't have been more wrong...

'Let me guess—more glitz and glamour!' Zak snorted in disgust as he read her thoughts. 'That isn't who I am, Tyler, it's what people like you make me out to be!'

People like her...

But she wasn't like those other reporters who would do anything for a story. That was the problem. If she had uncovered nothing else this week, she had at least realized that about herself. And if she were to leave here with any of her dignity intact, then she had to go now—before she made a complete idiot of herself and started blubbing all over the place again!

She smiled a little sadly. 'Unfortunately, glitz and glamour are what the readers of *The Daily Informer* like to read with their Sunday morning cereal and toast. You simply don't measure up to your pre-publicity, Zak.'

Ouch! That had hurt her to say, so heaven knew how Zak felt about it. If the tightening of his mouth, and the dangerous narrowing of his eyes were anything to go by, then not very good!

'I can honestly say that you don't measure up to yours, either,' he scorned. 'And I'm not referring to the fact that you weren't the man I was originally expecting!'

Ouch, again! On a more personal level this time. It was definitely time for her to go, before this conversation developed into a slanging match.

She feigned an unconcerned shrug. 'Then I guess we were both disappointed, weren't we?'

He nodded, a nerve pulsing in his rock-hard jaw. 'I guess we were.'

Tyler swallowed hard, knowing she had succeeded in what she had set out to do; if only alienating Zak like this didn't hurt so much! 'I'd better go, then,' she muttered.

'I think you better had,' Zak agreed icily before turning away from her.

Tyler gave one last, longing glance at the long length of that back turned so uncompromisingly towards her, knowing she hadn't just terminated her interview with Zak, that she had also effectively ended her career as a reporter. Before it had even begun, really.

She left the hotel suite, not knowing where she was going or what she was going to do now...

'Why are you looking so down in the mouth, Zak?' his brother Rik asked as he walked into Stazy's kitchen.

Zak glanced up from where he had been staring unseeingly into his empty coffee mug. 'When did you get back from France?'

'It's good to see you too!' Rik retorted sarcastically. 'And I got back a couple of hours ago, if you're really interested. Which, I suspect, you're really not,' he said astutely as he sat down opposite Zak at the kitchen table.

'Stazy didn't mention you were back,' Zak frowned. Although considering he'd been in this morose mood ever since he'd arrived half an hour ago, that wasn't really so surprising! 'And it is good to see you,' he added, trying to smile and at the same time doing his best to shake off his despondent mood.

His hotel suite had suddenly seemed small and oppressive after Tyler had left earlier, and so with nothing else to do, and nowhere else to go, Zak had come round to see Stazy. Their sister was upstairs at the moment bathing her baby son, Sam.

'How was Paris?' he asked Rik, more for something to say, really, than because he was actually interested.

Rik grinned. 'As beautiful and inspirational as ever.

I was on such a roll with this new screenplay I'm writing that I didn't really want to break off and leave,' he added wistfully.

Zak knew that, for some reason, Rik always worked well in Paris, that he loved everything about the place; which was why, when he was working on a new screenplay, he invariably chose to go there to do it.

'Then why did you?' he asked, making patterns in the sugar-bowl with his spoon now.

Where was Tyler now? Zak wondered. Had she so much as given him a second thought after leaving the hotel earlier? Or was she, having given up on this exclusive with him, already hot on the trail of some other so-called star? Someone a bit more cooperative than he had been, perhaps!

The latter probably, he decided with a heavy sigh. How could his life, the bachelor life he had always enjoyed to the full, suddenly seem so empty and point-less? Even the anticipation of the movie he was due to start work on next week didn't particularly interest him.

'What?' he questioned sharply, having glanced up to find Rik quietly watching him, dark brows raised.

'The première of *Gunslinger*,' Rik announced. 'Sat-urday. That's why I came back. I was the screenwriter, remember?'

'Oh. Yeah.' Zak gave an awkward grimace.

How could he have forgotten that Rik had written the screenplay to his last film? He was afraid he knew the answer to that only too well: because Tyler com-pletely occupied all his thoughts—how she looked, how she talked, how much he loved her!

'What's wrong, Zak?' his brother probed gently.

He stiffened immediately. 'Why should you imagine there's anything wrong?'

'Oh, come on, Zak,' Rik reproved. 'I'm your brother, okay. I know when there's something wrong. You aren't your usual cheerful self, for one thing,' he continued as Zak would have protested again. 'In fact, I would go so far as to say—hey, this doesn't have anything to do with your "mystery lady", does it?' he pounced with a speculative raise of an eyebrow. 'It does have something to do with her!' He grinned as Zak scowled blackly. 'Who is she, Zak? Anyone that I know? Or that I'm going to know...?'

'Leave it alone, Rik,' Zak growled, blue eyes narrowed in warning.

'Leave what alone?' Stazy enquired as she returned from successfully bathing her young son and putting him in his cot for his afternoon nap.

'I was just asking Zak about the "mystery lady",' Rik answered.

'Tyler?' Stazy frowned as she turned from pouring herself a mug of coffee. 'What about her?'

Was it Zak's imagination or did Stazy suddenly look a little uncomfortable? No, he was sure he wasn't imagining it; there was a definite frown between Stazy's troubled grey eyes.

'I think Zak is actually in love,' Rik said as he stared at him in astonishment; all of Zak's family were aware of his reluctance to get seriously involved with anyone.

But it hadn't been reluctance exactly, Zak realized now. It had been more to do with the fact that he had never met the right woman before. Before Tyler...

'In love? With Tyler?' Stazy's voice rose in agitation as she looked at him with some concern now. 'I thought the two of you seemed—quite friendly, last night, but she assured me that— Zak, it isn't a good idea for you to get involved with Tyler. I—you—she isn't quite what she seems.'

Zak studied his sister through narrowed eyes. Stazy was obviously seriously anxious about something. And if it involved Tyler, then he wanted to know what it was. More than that, he *needed* to know what it was!

'Then what is she?' he asked, every inch of his body tense as he waited for Stazy's answer.

'I—she—' Stazy broke off awkwardly. 'I promised her I wouldn't talk about it—wouldn't tell you about it, unless I thought your not knowing was going to hurt you in some way.'

Zak stood up suddenly, staring at his sister incredulously. 'Stazy, you've known me for all of your twenty-two years. I'm your brother, for goodness' sake, and yet you're telling me that in spite of all that you've chosen to keep the confidence of a woman you *only met for the first time last night*?' His voice rose in volume the longer he talked without taking a break, so that his final few words actually came out as an accusing shout. And he never shouted. Had never found anything disturbing enough in his adult life to shout about.

A fact Stazy was well aware of, if her startled expression was anything to go by. 'It wasn't like that,' she defended herself heatedly. 'You told me—you both said— Zak, is Rik right? Are you in love with Tyler?'

His jaw clenched as he gritted his teeth. 'And if I am?' he finally grated through barely moving lips.

'Oh, Zak, no!' Stazy groaned. 'I realized who she

really was the moment I met her last night. And she didn't deny it when I challenged her upstairs.'

'Hey, don't cry, Stazy.' Rik stood up to go to their sister as she looked in danger of doing exactly that.

Great, just great! Zak thought; he had now succeeded in reducing both the women he loved to tears in one single day!

'You couldn't have known, Stazy,' he tried to soothe his sister, feeling like a complete heel now. 'I didn't discover myself how I really felt about her until this morning. But if I'm understanding you correctly, you're telling me that Tyler isn't really Tyler?'

That was something he didn't understand at all. How could Tyler not be Tyler? And if she wasn't Tyler, then who the hell was she?

CHAPTER THIRTEEN

'AND so, you see, Tyler, the only reason I spoke to you the other evening was because I wanted to thank you,' Jane Morrow told her happily.

Tyler stared at the other woman in disbelief. True to her promise to Zak earlier, she had finally managed to track Jane Morrow down to the literary agency she now worked for, the two women going to a coffee bar nearby so that they could talk privately.

Only for the other woman to turn around and actually thank her for getting her sacked from her last job because she absolutely loved her new one!

Tyler frowned. 'You aren't angry? Resentful? Vengeful?' she probed.

'Heavens, no.' The other woman laughed. 'Of course I was all of those things at the time.' She grimaced ruefully. 'But I love what I'm doing now, and if I hadn't literally been given the push then I wouldn't be doing it.' She blushed slightly. 'There's also a man in the office who—well, my life has completely turned around, I can assure you. Which was why I tried to thank you when I saw you at O'Malley's on Tuesday.'

Unfortunately, this also meant that Jane Morrow wasn't the person responsible for the gossip, setting David Miller on them, or the photograph!

Then who was? Tyler was at a complete loss. The only consolation—if it could be called that!—was that now she had terminated her interview with Zak, perhaps those other things would stop too.

Zak...

God, how just thinking about him made her heart ache!

Enough for her to wish she hadn't turned down the chance of an affair with him?

Oh, yes! In fact, since she had left his hotel a couple of hours ago, she had twice turned around with the intention of going back, apologizing for the things she had said, and telling him she had made a mistake about having a relationship with him, however temporary.

It was always when she reached this part of her apology that she stopped herself from doing any such thing.

As Zak had pointed out so succinctly, he hadn't actually asked her to have an affair with him, so how could she go back and tell him she was more than willing, after all?

She couldn't. And after all those things she had said to him, those deliberately hurtful things, she couldn't ask him to resume the interview, either.

Besides, the interview wasn't something she wanted to do any more. She had realized, at some point during that hurtful conversation with Zak this morning, that she couldn't do this, that dredging up secrets and scandals in other people's lives, and then making them public, wasn't for her. That reporting wasn't for her...

A part of the reason for that decision, she knew, was because someone had been doing exactly that to Zak and herself the last few days, and she had found it despicable.

Oh, she had received her fair share of publicity as Tyler Harwood but, probably because of Rufus's influence, it had never been of a scandalous or hurtful nature; the hounding of the last few days had been both those things.

Quite what she was going to do next, stay in England or return to the States, she had no idea yet, but her time at *The Daily Informer* was definitely at an end.

Which was why, when Zak walked into the newsroom of the paper an hour later, she was in the middle of clearing all her personal belongings from her desk!

She could feel her face pale as she watched him stride across the room, tersely acknowledging a couple of reporters who said hello to him, while at the same time his razor-sharp gaze remained firmly fixed on Tyler.

What was he doing here? She had thought after this morning that she would never see him again, except on a movie screen, and yet three hours after they had parted so badly, here he was.

But perhaps he wasn't here to see her? He had come to see Bill Graham the last time, so perhaps—

'Tyler *Harwood*, isn't it?' he snarled as he came to a halt beside her desk.

Tyler instantly felt her legs go weak at the knees. He knew. How? His sister must have told him…

Zak looked at her coldly, his gaze raking over her with obvious contempt. 'I have absolutely no idea what game you've been playing with me, Miss Harwood—'

'Tyler,' she interjected, her lips feeling numb. If only her heart felt the same way! 'Didn't Stazy tell you? Explain why—'

'My sister,' he cut in icily, 'trusting soul that she is, is of the opinion that there are certain—aspects, of your pretence, that you should tell me yourself!' His acidic tone told Tyler exactly what he thought of that!

He was angry, and Tyler knew he had a perfect right to be with her. But not with his sister. Stazy wasn't the one who deserved Zak's justifiable fury.

'I was the one who asked her to help me, okay?' Tyler told him fiercely. 'And she assured me that she would only do so as long as it didn't hurt you.'

'Speculative gossip and damning photographs didn't qualify as that to you, hmm?' Zak growled.

He couldn't *still* think Tyler was in some way responsible for those things? But what could she tell him to convince him otherwise? Jane Morrow was so obviously out of the equation now, and Tyler had no one else to pin it on. And already lying to Zak about her identity wasn't exactly the best way to go about convincing him she hadn't lied to him about anything else either!

Zak looked disgusted. 'No wonder you were so upset this morning by my phone call with Max in Los Angeles; did you think he was going to expose you for who you really are?'

She flinched at his disparaging tone. 'Hardly,' she came back flatly. 'LA isn't somewhere I go too often!'

'Not glitzy and glamorous enough for the rich society darling of New York?' Zak returned pointedly.

Their obviously heated conversation was attracting quite a lot of attention, a hush having fallen over the newsroom ever since Zak had stalked in.

So much so that Bill Graham was curious enough to wander over to his open office door. 'Twice in one week, Zak?' he taunted the younger man. 'Careful, or I'll think you're playing favourites with my reporters.'

'I can't see a single reporter in this room I would

even give the time of day to!' Zak ground out, giving the other man a glacial glare, his hands clenched at his sides.

There was an audible gasp around the room, a certain hostility in the air now, too.

It was all her fault, Tyler realized dismally, knowing that it was her Zak was angry with, her he had directed that insulting remark to. But he had insulted every other reporter in the room to do it!

'Why don't you step into my office, Zak, and we can talk there?' Bill invited pleasantly, only those that knew him well able to recognize the steely edge to his tone. Tyler had come to know him quite well the last six months. Although not quite as well, she had discovered an hour or so ago, as she had thought she had…!

'Tyler can join us if she cares to,' Bill added persuasively as Zak made no move to join him.

She gave a fierce shake of her head. 'I won't if you don't mind, Bill, I still have some things to do here. But you two go right ahead,' she offered—and then she could make good her escape. Zak was pretty scary in this mood. Not that it wasn't wholly merited, but it was still scary!

His gaze speared her once more, before he turned back to the older man. 'Why not?' he bit out, not sparing Tyler so much as a second glance as he strode across to join Bill.

That was just fine with her! She wanted out of here, anyway. Even more so since Zak had just insulted half the people she had worked with for the last six months, all of them now looking at her with varying degrees of perplexity. And why not? They knew as well as she did that she was the reason Zak Prince had just been uncharacteristically rude to them.

The sooner she got out of here—and away from Zak—the better for everyone!

'Exactly what do you think you're doing, Zak?' Bill Graham queried as he closed the office door before moving to sit behind his desk.

Zak didn't answer, choosing instead to stride restlessly up and down the small confines of the room; his conversation with Tyler just now had left him feeling like a caged tiger who needed to bite someone!

To be truthful, he wasn't a hundred per cent certain what he was doing here himself. Except he had felt a need, after talking to Stazy, to at least let Tyler know the game was up.

Tyler Harwood. Pampered heiress. Society princess. The list of names the media had dubbed her was endless.

He should perhaps have guessed something didn't quite add up about Tyler Wood—her friendship with Gerald Knight, for one thing, the Vera Wang dress for another; they were hardly in keeping with the junior reporter she was supposed to be. Hell, he had guessed there was something different about her, just not the full extent of that difference!

And why was he so furious about it? Because she had lied to him? Hidden a huge part of herself from him? Did that make her other than the woman he had fallen in love with? He didn't know!

Bill tried again. 'Unless I'm mistaken, you were giving Tyler a hard time just now.'

Zak gave a derisive snort. 'I want to shake her until her teeth rattle!'

Bill pulled a face. 'Oh, I think you shook her up quite enough—without getting physical about it!'

Zak glowered down at the older man. 'She made a fool out of me! She made a fool out of you, too,' he pointed out. 'Do you have any idea who she really is?'

'I know exactly who she is, Zak,' Bill revealed softly. 'I've always known.'

Zak blinked, stopping the pacing to stare at the other man now. Bill Graham *knew*—

'Sit down, Zak.' Bill sighed wearily. 'Please,' he added as Zak didn't move.

He dropped down into the chair on the opposite side of the desk, still more livid than he'd ever been in his life.

'Better,' Bill approved. 'Now let's set the record straight. Of course I know who Tyler is; her only qualification as editor of her college newspaper certainly didn't merit me going to all the trouble of taking her on as a junior reporter! No, I did that as a favour to an old friend.' He shrugged. 'But, you know, Tyler surprised me,' he continued. 'She's good, Zak. Maybe not as a reporter on a tabloid newspaper,' he conceded ruefully. 'But her style of writing is excellent.'

'I wouldn't know,' Zak muttered.

The other man gave him a frown. 'Thirty years ago, when we actually reported the news and not this rubbish about who's sleeping with who this week, Tyler would have become a star reporter. Putting it bluntly, she's too good a writer to waste her talents on a newspaper like this one. Besides,' he added with a small smile, 'she has a conscience.'

Zak didn't want to hear that, or what a good writer she was; he was still too angry with her for that. 'You said you employed Tyler initially as a favour to an old friend...?' he prompted shrewdly.

'So I did.' Bill gave a laughing acknowledgement of that shrewdness. 'Tyler's father Rufus Harwood is a very old friend. I owe him more than one. He called me, explained about Tyler being in London looking for a job; I hired her.'

Rufus Harwood was someone Zak had heard of, a media mogul of mega proportions. He owned a television network in the USA, several radio stations, plus several newspapers.

Zak shook his head. 'But how could he possibly know, when Tyler walked out claiming she was going to make it as a reporter—' at least Stazy had confided some things in him! '—that she would come to this paper to get a job?'

'He couldn't,' Bill admitted. 'But Rufus was pretty sure she wouldn't get a job without proper experience on any other paper—and he was right! Even I wouldn't have given her a job without Rufus's request. As predicted, she was turned down by quite a few before she came here. And you know the rest!'

Rufus Harwood. Tyler's father. An extremely powerful man, not to be taken lightly, if the publicity about him was to be believed. And Zak had no reason to believe it wasn't. Why else would his only child decide to leave her home, her country, in order to become her own person and try to make it by herself?

Zak couldn't fault her for doing that. Only for using him, deceiving him, in order to do it.

'I was just lucky she came here,' Bill continued seriously. 'She's a lovely woman, Zak. Stubborn too, of course,' he added with more than a touch of admiration. 'She wasn't at all happy with the man Rufus picked out for her to marry.'

Marry? Tyler was *engaged*?

Zak must have looked as though he was about to do somebody some serious physical damage, because Bill said hurriedly, 'I said she wasn't happy, Zak. In fact she totally rejected any idea of marrying Richard Astor-Wilson.' He chuckled. 'That must have really upset Rufus!'

'Richard Astor-Wilson?' Zak choked.

That was yet another name he knew. Old family. Old money. One of the most powerful families in New York. And Tyler had refused to marry the only son and heir!

'Can you believe it?' Bill nodded as he saw Zak's expression. 'You have to like and admire Tyler just for doing that.' He sighed. 'It's a pity she's leaving. I'm going to miss—'

'She's leaving?' Zak echoed sharply.

'In fact, she was clearing her desk when you arrived—' He broke off as Zak stood up to walk over to the internal windows and look out into the main newsroom.

Tyler was nowhere to be seen. The desk where she had been sitting when he'd arrived was completely empty too.

'She messed up with that story on your brother Nik and his girlfriend—now his wife, of course.' Bill shrugged as Zak turned back to him accusingly. 'Plus she didn't deliver the story on you, either,' he added, eyeing Zak challengingly.

'So you just *fired* her?' Zak exploded.

Tyler had gone? To God knew where—because he certainly didn't!

'No, I did *not* fire her.' Bill bristled irritably. 'She may have thought I was going to, though. She was on a warning to dig up as much fodder for the gossip columns on you as she could, or she was out,' he explained. 'I was never going to do it, of course, but—'

'Because you *owed* Rufus Harwood!' Zak gibed.

'I just wanted to prove to her that she was in the wrong line of work.'

Tyler was gone! It was really all that Zak could think about at the moment. 'Did she know you only employed her initially because of who her father is?'

'She does now,' Bill replied.

Zak frowned. 'But not before?'

Bill quirked greying brows. 'What do you think?'

'I think—' Zak spoke between his teeth '—that if she had known, she would have told you to go to hell and your job along with you!'

'There you go.' The older man gave a satisfied smile. 'You know she's a good kid, too. So why are you giving her such a hard time?'

Zak opened his mouth to answer the other man, and then closed it again. Why *was* he giving her such a hard time?

Because she had lied to him about who she really was? Zak supposed she hadn't exactly lied—she had just been economical with the truth. Or was the real reason he was so angry because he had fallen in love with her, and she didn't return those feelings? Yes, that was probably closer to the truth!

'I didn't sack her, Zak,' Bill Graham repeated quietly. 'She resigned, effective immediately, because she couldn't bring herself to write that story on Nik and Jinx last month. Because, in spite of believing I was going to sack her if she didn't come up with some juicy gossip about you, she couldn't do that either. I told you, the girl has a conscience.'

Zak frowned. 'So there actually was no exclusive article for the Sunday magazine? No feature piece?'

'Nope,' the other man confirmed. 'I'm afraid that what *The Daily Informer* does best is scandal!'

Now Zak was totally confused. Tyler must have felt pretty strongly about making it on her own to have gone to the lengths she had, to have given up all the pampered luxury she was used to, the social recognition, to become a junior reporter on a less-than-reputable newspaper, using the tube for transport, living in a small apartment. And, at a guess, not always having the money to eat properly...

But given two assignments by her editor, first the story on Nik and Jinx, and now another one on him, Tyler had not written either and had simply packed up her things and left. Because her *emotions* were involved?

Zak fervently hoped that, where he was concerned, Tyler getting emotionally involved was a really good sign...

'I may not have sacked Tyler, Zak, but I did have reason to sack someone else this morning,' Bill Graham interrupted his thoughts.

Zak's interest sharpened, deepening further at the pointed way the other man returned his gaze. 'Morgan...?' he guessed.

Bill gave a humourless smile. 'Morgan.' He nodded, his mouth tightening. 'If anyone asks me I shall say he resigned for personal reasons, but within these four walls...? I don't take kindly to one of my staff giving stories and photographs to rival newspapers!'

'So Perry Morgan was responsible for the gossip about the ''mystery lady'' in my life? But why would he do something like that to Tyler? I thought the two of them were friends.' More than friends, he recalled jealously.

'It wasn't aimed at Tyler, Zak, it was aimed at you,' Bill said. 'He's in love with Tyler—I'm pretty sure she doesn't return the feeling,' Bill assured him. 'If she did, none of this would have happened.'

'I don't understand you.'

Bill sighed. 'He muttered something about a photograph he accidentally took of you and Tyler, that you were annoyed about it, and had told Tyler so in no uncertain terms. I think he reasoned—if it can be called that!—that if he could cause enough of a rift between you, if you thought it was Tyler responsible for those things, that he could stop any sort of—friendship, shall we say?—developing between the two of you. Did he succeed?' Bill asked with more than a touch of mockery.

'Only up to a point,' Zak admitted, remembering the accusations he had hurled at Tyler after each of those incidents. Totally undeserved accusations, it now seemed...

'I'm not even going to ask where you're going.' The seasoned editor laughed as Zak moved towards the door. 'Tell her she should write a book.'

'What?'

'Tell Tyler she should write a book. A biography, maybe. Her research is excellent, her style of writing even more so. Tell her to write Rufus's biography.' Bill grinned wickedly. 'Rufus would love that!'

Zak gave a rueful shake of his head, once again turning to leave, before stopping again, his expression rather pained as he turned back to the other man. 'I don't have Tyler's address,' he admitted irritably.

He wasn't sure that admission merited quite that amount of laughter from the other man!

CHAPTER FOURTEEN

TYLER stared apprehensively at her apartment door as the knock sounded for a second time.

Could it be Zak come to insult her some more? Well, she couldn't take any more today. She already felt so brittle she was in danger of snapping in two. One more insult from him and she was likely to do exactly that!

Today had already been so awful. So awful that, apart from a single telephone call when she'd got in, and a half-hearted attempt to pack a suitcase, she hadn't had the energy to accomplish anything else towards leaving.

'Tyler? Are you in there?' Perry's voice asked through the door. 'Open the door if you are; I really need to talk to you.'

It was Perry. Not Zak.

But of course it wasn't Zak, she derided herself even as she moved to answer the door; Zak had already said everything to her that he needed to say!

'Tyler!' Perry greeted her with obvious relief as she opened the door. 'What's going on?' he demanded as he followed her into the apartment. 'You didn't call me about lunch, and when I telephoned the paper Kelly told me that you'd been sacked.'

'Resigned,' Tyler corrected wearily. 'I resigned, I wasn't sacked,' she explained as he still looked puzzled.

'But—where are you going?' Perry frowned as he spotted the partly packed suitcase in her bedroom.

She moved to close the bedroom door. 'Home, I thought.' She attempted to smile.

'You were just going to pack up and go?' he said indignantly. 'Without telling me?'

'Of course not.' She sighed, not sure that was exactly the truth.

Perry had been the last thing on her mind today, hence her having completely forgotten to telephone him about having lunch together. Oh, she probably would have thought about calling him to say goodbye. Eventually.

'I'm not leaving right this minute,' she said flatly.

'I don't see why you have to go at all,' Perry objected. 'I—Tyler, I've resigned too—'

'Oh, Perry, no!' She groaned, knowing her own resignation had to be responsible for that. It was bad enough that her life had turned upside down; she didn't want to be responsible for messing up Perry's life too.

He shrugged. 'I don't want to continue working at the paper if you aren't there too.'

She already was responsible, she realized. This situation just seemed to be getting worse and worse.

'Look, I don't see why you have to go anywhere, Tyler,' Perry was saying eagerly. 'We can go freelance. In fact, this just might be the opportunity we've both been looking for— What do you mean, no?' he snapped as Tyler simply shook her head at his suggestion.

'Perry, I haven't been completely honest with you. I'm not who you think I am. My name isn't even

Wood. I—my father is Rufus Harwood,' she told him reluctantly.

'I already know that.' He waved a hand in dismissal of her revelation. 'You—'

'You do?' Tyler was stunned. Perry knew?

'Of course. I'm not completely stupid, you know. I recognized you within days of you coming to work at the paper,' he said. 'It doesn't have to change anything; I'll simply come back to America with you, if that's where you want to go. Once your father sees how much in love with you I am, then I'm sure he'll give his consent to—'

'Perry, stop!' Tyler cried; hadn't he heard anything she'd said to him the other day after he'd told her he was in love with her? Obviously not.

And it was more than a little disquieting to realize that Perry had known exactly who she was all along...

'You can't possibly be in love with me; you don't even know me,' she protested.

She couldn't believe the irony—such a short time ago she'd told Zak that he didn't know her either...not that he'd claimed he was in love with her!

Zak.

She had to stop thinking about him! Otherwise she was going to go quietly insane. But one thing was for certain: loving Zak as she did, she couldn't even give Perry the ghost of a hope that she would ever return his feelings.

'I'm sorry, Perry, I really am. But I—I'm going home alone.' It was going to be traumatic enough as it was, without dragging Perry into it.

He stared at her for several moments, and then he gave a thoughtful nod of his head. 'You're right, that's probably the best way to go about this. You can ex-

plain the situation to your family, and then I can join
you in a couple of days—'

'Perry, you aren't listening to me!' she interrupted,
upset that he was being so persistent. 'I—I'm not in
love with you—'

'Of course you are,' he contradicted. 'You've just
become a little confused the last few days. It's all Zak
Prince's fault.' He scowled at the mention of the other
man. 'The two of us were getting along really well
until he came along. And we'll—'

'Perry, no!' The more he continued in this vein the
more agitated she was becoming. 'I'm really not in
love with you. I like you very much. You've been a
good friend to me since I came here, but I—' Her
words were cut off as Perry pulled her into his arms
and tried to kiss her.

It was the end of the line for Tyler, and she finally
started to get angry with him. She didn't want this.
Didn't return his feelings. And she never would.

She wrenched her mouth away from his, pushing
hard against his chest in an effort to release herself. 'I
said *no*, Perry! And I meant it!' Her earlier unease,
when he'd told her that he had known who she was
all this time, returned as she saw the determination on
his face as he glowered down at her.

'It's him, isn't it?' Perry accused, his good-looking
face becoming positively menacing in his anger.

She swallowed hard. 'I don't know what you mean,
but for the sake of our friendship—'

'It isn't friendship I want from you!' he snapped.
'You know what I want—' He broke off as a knock
sounded on the apartment door, his expression becoming even uglier.

Tyler felt overwhelming relief at the interruption.

She didn't care who was on the other side of that door: the landlord asking for his rent, someone conducting a survey, or even someone trying to sell her something—she just wanted to kiss whoever it was. Perry was frightening in this mood, and had become a man she didn't even recognize. There was also the fact that he had always known her real identity to contend with...

'Is that him now?' Perry asked as she moved to open the door. 'Zak Prince on his white charger come to rescue the fair maiden?' he jeered unpleasantly.

She wished that it were Zak, even while she told herself that it wasn't. But a door-to-door salesman might not be enough for her to get Perry out of her apartment.

'Zak!' Tyler stared incredulously up at the man as he stood grim-faced on the other side of the door, that grimness increasing as he looked past her into the apartment and saw Perry there.

'Tyler.' He nodded tersely, the expression in his eyes unreadable. 'I haven't caught you at an inconvenient moment, have I?'

Despite the edge of sarcasm to his tone, Tyler could still have laughed with the relief at his being here. 'Not at all. Come inside.' She grasped his arm and practically pulled him into the apartment, only to find herself standing awkwardly between the two men as they glared at each other.

She had no idea what Zak was doing here, and really didn't care if it was only to level fresh accusations at her; he was here, and now she could perhaps get Perry, who had turned into such a stranger, to leave.

'You aren't wanted here, Prince,' Perry announced suddenly.

Tyler gasped at his insulting tone. Not only was it incredibly rude, it was also patently untrue; she so *did* want Zak here!

But Zak didn't look at all perturbed by the other man's aggressive tone, his expression slightly softened as he looked down at her. 'Is that true, Tyler?' he asked softly. 'Do you want me to go?'

'No!' she responded sharply, and then forced herself to take a deep breath and calm down. 'No, of course I don't,' she answered more calmly. 'Actually, Perry, I thought you were the one who was leaving?' She looked at him challengingly.

He raised dark brows. 'Hardly,' he drawled, reaching out to pull her against his side, his arm moving possessively about her waist. 'As it happens, Prince, you're here just in time to offer us your congratulations; Tyler has just agreed to marry me.'

Tyler stared up at him in consternation, more and more convinced that Perry had only become her friend because of who she really was.

Because he couldn't honestly think that she—

There was no way that she had ever agreed—

He just couldn't be serious!

But she could see, by the tight clenching of his jaw, the dangerous glitter in his eyes, that he was. Deadly serious.

Zak felt as if someone had just punched him in the stomach. Tyler couldn't be going to marry this man. If she was going to marry anyone, it was going to be *him*!

Now he really did feel as if someone had just knocked all the air from his lungs! He had never even contemplated marrying anyone before, and now, in the space of four days, he knew that his life would never be complete again if it didn't have Tyler in it, as his wife. That he would never be wholly alive again if she married another man!

And then he caught sight of the expression on Tyler's face: disbelief mixed with dismay. Hardly the look of a woman who had just agreed to marry the man she loved!

Zak straightened. 'Really? Then Tyler must have a very forgiving nature,' he said in a hard voice.

Perry's arm tightened about Tyler's waist; it was enough to make Zak feel like hitting him!

'What do you mean?' Tyler asked, a little confused.

Zak glared at the other man. 'Do you want to tell her or shall I?'

An angry flush darkened Perry's cheeks. 'I have no idea what you're talking about,' he protested.

'Neither do I, Zak.' Tyler still sounded confused.

If Perry Morgan didn't stop touching Tyler in that intimately possessive way soon, Zak knew he wasn't going to be responsible for his actions!

He thrust his hands into the pockets of his denims to keep them out of mischief. 'Only that your friend here is the one responsible for that article and photograph of us appearing in those newspapers. Or didn't he tell you that?' he added softly as he saw Tyler turn to stare incredulously at the other man.

Tyler finally moved out of the other man's grasp—instantly lessening the pain in Zak's chest. 'Is this true, Perry?'

'Of course it isn't true,' Perry scorned. 'He's just telling you that to try and drive a wedge between us. Prince probably organized it himself—people like him thrive on publicity so much that they have to create their own!'

So far Zak had held off hitting the other man because he wasn't sure how Tyler would react to him doing that, but at this precise moment he was in danger of forgetting all about that and hitting Perry Morgan, anyway!

'Strange,' he grated, his hands bunched into fists now. 'That isn't the way Bill Graham tells it.'

'Bill?' Tyler echoed, looking very pale now. 'But what—?'

'Just ignore him, Tyler,' Perry Morgan cut in angrily. 'Bill Graham wouldn't give him the time of day, let alone tell him anything of such a personal nature!'

But as Zak and Tyler both knew, Bill had talked to him, not once, but twice, and he could see the memory of this morning's meeting, of the two men being together in Bill's office when she'd left, in her wide brown eyes.

'What do you think, Tyler? Did Bill Graham tell me he'd fired this guy or didn't he?' Zak arched blond brows in query.

Tyler looked as if she couldn't take much more, and when Zak thought of all she had already gone through this morning—the photograph in the newspaper, the argument with him, leaving the paper—he really wasn't surprised she looked slightly punch-drunk. He wished he could make this easier for her, but, if nothing else, she needed to know the truth about Perry Morgan.

She swallowed hard. 'I believe you when you say he did,' she said, moving away from Perry as he momentarily relaxed his hold. She turned to glare at him. 'What I find hard to believe is that you did those things, Perry!' Her voice shook with anger and her eyes flashed. 'And you told me you'd resigned because you didn't want to continue working there without me! I think you'd better leave right now.'

Perry Morgan's face flushed angrily. 'But we're getting married—'

'We most certainly are *not*!' Tyler snapped. 'We never were. Even if you hadn't done those awful things, I still wouldn't marry you. I already told you, I don't love you.'

Zak felt such relief at hearing these words, and looked admiringly at Tyler. He knew it was something of a cliché, but she really did look magnificent when she was angry, all five feet two inches of her proudly tense, the colour in her cheeks adding depth and sparkle to those beautiful brown eyes. And for once it wasn't him she was angry with!

'I suppose you think Tyler *Harwood* is too high and mighty to marry a mere photographer!' Perry Morgan sneered nastily, obviously realizing he had completely lost any chance of a relationship with her.

Tyler gave him a scathing glance. 'Make that *ex*-photographer! If I know Bill you'll be lucky to get a job working for the *Hicksville Chronicle* photographing baby shows! As for me,' she went on to ram the point home, 'I never had any intention of marrying you, either as Tyler Wood or Tyler Harwood!' She frowned. 'Admit it, it's only because you knew who I was all the time that you became my friend in the first place!'

Zak felt for her as her voice shook emotionally, knew how much this must have hurt her.

Perry Morgan gave her a thoroughly unpleasant smile. 'Why else would I bother with a junior reporter—and not a very good one, at that?'

'It's time for you to go—past time!' Tyler looked

at the man with cold, compelling eyes as she walked over and held the door open for him. 'And don't bother to find your way back. Ever!' she bit out icily as Perry Morgan walked jauntily across the room.

'You know, you really are a—'

'Just go, Morgan!' Zak snarled as the other man seemed about to launch into some verbal abuse that Tyler could very well do without.

He watched tensely as Perry did exactly that, ready to leap to Tyler's defence if the other man should so much as try to talk to her again. In fact, Zak was inwardly somewhat disappointed that he didn't; hitting Perry Morgan would have been a pleasure!

Tyler closed the door firmly, taking several seconds to compose herself before turning back to face Zak. 'Thank you,' she murmured huskily. 'I still can't believe he—but I should have known.' She sighed. 'He was the one to introduce me to David Miller a few months back. I guess I just didn't want to think that Perry had sold me out.' She looked at him apologetically. 'I really believed, until a short time ago, that it was Jane Morrow who was responsible for setting the press on us. I didn't want to mention her name before because—well, I'm sure you understand why I didn't...'

Zak took a surprised breath. Jane Morrow! *That* was who that blonde who'd come up to them outside O'Malley's on Monday night was! It was no wonder he hadn't recognized her immediately—the only time he'd been introduced to her was when he'd bumped into Nik having dinner with her, some weeks before Nik had met his wife.

Tyler shook her head. 'What could Perry possibly have hoped to achieve by doing those things?'

Was this the time to put forward Bill Graham's theory: that Perry Morgan had sensed the deepening feeling between her and Zak, and was determined to put a stop to it? Would Tyler be ready to hear that just yet?

Zak shrugged. 'I guess he was jealous of the time you were spending with me.'

Her eyes widened. 'But that was work. Business.'

Work. Business. The two words hit Zak like a slap in the face. Was that all he was to Tyler—work and business?

'Perhaps he really was in love with you?' Zak grated.

Her eyes flashed chocolate-brown fire. 'My father's money and prestige is what he was in love with! If that's his idea of love, he can keep it!'

It wasn't how Zak loved her, no. He just wanted to be with her every minute of the day and night, to share everything with her, to know and cherish everything about her, to have her cherish and love him in the same way...

'So what will you do now?' he asked. 'Bill tells me you've resigned from the paper.'

'I've already called my father and made my peace with him. I'm going home.'

'Before or after our date on Saturday?'

Tyler's eyes widened. 'You still want me to go to the première with you?'

'Why not?' He forced his reply to sound casual. 'It's a bit short notice to ask anyone else at this late date,' he added so that she wouldn't think he was about to go all domineering on her as Perry Morgan had.

She gave a rueful smile. 'That's honest, at least.

And after Perry's deceit—' her mouth tightened at the mention of the other man '—I need that. So, yes, I would love to attend the première with you.' She gave him a shaky smile. 'As Tyler Harwood, if that's okay with you?'

She could go as Tyler Smith as long as she went with him! Zak inwardly acknowledged with a definite lift of spirits. 'Fine. Oh, before I go...I have some words of wisdom for you from Bill.'

She looked wary now. 'Yes?'

Zak smiled reassuringly. 'He said to tell you your writing is too good for the tabloid press, and that you should write a book. A biography. He suggested your father as the subject of that biography.'

He was completely captivated as Tyler burst out laughing. 'Oh, Rufus would love that! He would probably disinherit me just for suggesting it!' Her eyes glowed mischievously. 'He's always said that the only good biographies are the ones that aren't written. In fact, he...' She trailed off, her expression thoughtful now. 'You know, it's actually not such a bad idea,' she said slowly. 'Although getting my father to agree to it could be interesting!'

'Think about it,' Zak suggested softly, happier now that he knew he would at least see Tyler again on Saturday evening. 'You could always write one on me first just to show him how good you are.'

Where the hell had that idea come from? He was about as keen to have his biography written as he was to have a tooth extracted! Except that having Tyler write his biography would mean he could keep her in his life for several more weeks, months, years...

'You?' Tyler looked as stunned at the suggestion as he had felt making it.

'Why not?' Zak shrugged.

'You can still ask me that after the disaster of the last four days?'

He wanted to ask her a lot more than that! And with the time he might have bought himself with the idea of her writing his biography, perhaps he could do just that.

'None of that was your fault. And to give you something to think about,' he added, walking over to the door now, 'that night at O'Malley's, when I was—less than polite to the waiter?'

'Yes?' she responded warily.

'The reason I reacted so badly to the disappearance of the duck that I usually ordered from the menu was because I'm severely dyslexic. I could probably have figured out some of the other dishes on the menu given time—but it would have been too obvious to you and everyone else that I was having problems reading. So I stuck to the easy option and just ordered a steak instead.'

Zak didn't give her a chance to make a reply before letting himself out of the apartment and closing the door quietly behind him.

It was time for the trust between them to begin...

CHAPTER FIFTEEN

'WHY did you tell me that about yourself?'

'Tell you what?' Zak asked innocently.

Tyler sat beside him in the back of the white chauffeur-driven limousine he had arrived in to pick her up for the première, the glass partition between them and the driver firmly closed.

Zak looked absolutely wonderful in his tuxedo, completely relaxed as he lounged in the seat beside her.

Tyler had been wondering for the last two days why he had suddenly told her on Thursday about his dyslexia. She knew that it wasn't public knowledge, that it was exactly the kind of juicy gossip she had been searching for in order to keep her job at *The Daily Informer*. That would probably still assure her a job there—if she wanted it. Which she didn't.

But that still didn't explain why Zak had confided in her in that sudden, unexpected way...

'Your dyslexia,' she reminded him, looking at him searchingly in the early-evening sunlight.

He shrugged. 'Another of my secrets is that I actually hate film premières! Acting is one thing, being the focus of all eyes, as myself, is something else.'

Why was he telling her these things, intensely private things? Was it just because of the biography he was suggesting she write about him?

Or was it something else?

She frowned, deciding there was only one way to find out...

'I hate caviare,' she revealed. 'And I had a lisp until I was ten, when an orthodontist, a brace, and a speech therapist sorted it out.'

Zak nodded in acknowledgement. 'I can't stand dill pickles in burgers. And I didn't kiss a girl until I was in tenth grade.'

'The girls at school called me Metal-mouth for two years. And I hate oysters.'

'My first date was a disaster; I threw up all over the girl at the top of a Ferris wheel. I hate squid.'

Tyler still had no idea where this was going, but she carried on anyway. Hoping! 'My first date was a disaster too; my mother insisted on coming along! I hate syrup on my pancakes.'

'Oh, now that's just going too far, Tyler,' Zak protested laughingly. 'No red-blooded American could possibly hate syrup on their pancakes!'

'I do,' she insisted. 'But I love strawberries and cream.'

'I love cold pizza for breakfast.'

'I love chocolate for breakfast.'

'I love English roast beef with all the trimmings.'

'I love something they call toad-in-the-hole. I know it sounds disgusting.' She laughed at his expression. 'But it's actually just sausages cooked in batter.'

'I prefer cricket to American baseball.'

'I love tennis more than either of them.'

'I love you.'

'I love— Zak?' Tyler stared up at him, wondering if she could possibly have just heard him correctly. Had Zak really said that he loved her?

'I didn't mean for it to come out quite like that,'

Zak muttered, shaking his head in self-disgust as he turned towards her in his car seat. 'I know this isn't the right time or place,' he added as they rapidly approached the theatre where his film was showing. 'I was going to show you this evening that being seen with me isn't all bad. Persuade you into perhaps staying on in England with the idea of writing my biography. And then, after a couple of weeks, I was going to—damn.' He groaned, raking his hand through his hair. 'It's true, Tyler, I do love you. But I'm not expecting—'

'I love you too, Zak,' she cut in shakily, wondering if she could possibly be dreaming all of this. 'I love you, too!' she repeated, her eyes glowing.

Zak's hands moved to cradle either side of her face as he looked intensely down at her. 'You do? You really do?' he asked uncertainly.

Tyler gave a choked laugh, encouraged by this uncertainty from a man who was always so self-assured. 'I've had a crush on you since I was fifteen years old!'

He made a face. 'I had a crush on Elizabeth Taylor when I was fifteen, but I didn't fall in love with her when I finally met her ten years ago!'

'Whereas I fell in love with you the moment I met you,' Tyler assured him.

Zak raised a mischievous eyebrow. 'You couldn't have done; I was rude and arrogant.'

'I loved you anyway,' Tyler insisted. 'I do love you, Zak. Very much,' she reiterated.

'Enough to marry me?' he probed gruffly, his gaze searching.

Her heart leapt just at the thought of being Zak's wife. But... 'You don't have to marry me if you don't want to,' she offered.

Zak grinned. 'Anything but marriage and your father would probably have me put in chains somewhere and throw away the key! In fact, I very much doubt whether he's going to be thrilled at the idea of having me for a son-in-law.'

Tyler shook her head. 'What my father really wants is grandchildren; I don't think he particularly cares who I marry in order for him to have them!' That was perhaps a slight exaggeration, but, after the long telephone conversations she had had with her father and mother over the last couple of days, she really did believe that as long as she was happy then her father would be happy for her. 'Besides—' she reached up and touched the hardness of Zak's clenched jaw '—this really has nothing to do with my father, Zak. Only you and me. Zak and Tyler.' God, how wonderful that sounded!

'Then marriage it is,' Zak declared firmly. 'How about we forget Tyler Wood and Tyler Harwood, and go for Tyler Prince instead?'

It sounded like heaven. Like all of her wishes coming true, she decided as Zak took her in his arms and began to kiss her.

Two days ago she had felt as if the bottom had dropped out of her world, just the thought of never seeing Zak again after tonight making her feel totally miserable. In fact, her crumbled dream of becoming a reporter had completely paled into insignificance in comparison with never seeing Zak again.

And now this!

It was so much more than she had ever hoped for. Zak loved her. She loved him. It was all that mattered.

Zak drew back reluctantly as the limousine pulled up in front of the theatre, accompanied by the sound of dozens of women screaming as they realized Zak was in this car.

Tyler wanted to scream with them, but settled for smiling proudly at his side as those women cheered and clapped as they walked the short distance into the theatre, camera bulbs flashing.

Zak's arm tightened about her waist. 'Your photograph is going to be splashed all over the front pages of the newspapers tomorrow,' he warned her.

Tyler shrugged. 'Who cares?' And she didn't. She would be happy to be photographed at Zak's side for the rest of her life.

'Richard Astor-Wilson might,' he teased.

Her eyes widened. 'You know about Richard too?'

Zak grinned. 'Bill Graham did. He and your father go way back, you know.'

'I do now. So much for striking out on my own, hmm?'

'But that's exactly what you did, Tyler,' Zak insisted. 'I'm sure Bill is serious about you writing a book.'

Tyler smiled. 'I've already mentioned it to my father. He's thinking about it.' She chuckled. 'That usually means yes! As for Richard...' She sighed. 'I'm afraid I wasn't very nice to him before I left New York.'

'Good,' Zak said with satisfaction.

She laughed. 'That's quite a fan club you have out there,' she murmured as the women could still be heard screaming Zak's name.

Zak's eyes were a deep, deep blue as he smiled down at her. 'A fan club of one is all I want,' he assured her huskily. 'As long as that one is you.'

'For always, Zak,' she promised as she reached up and kissed him.

'Always,' he vowed in return.

'Does the fact that the two of you can't seem to take your eyes off each other mean that I'm shortly to have another sister-in-law?'

Tyler turned curiously to the tall, dark-haired man who had spoken to them, instantly recognizing him as the youngest Prince brother, Rik.

Zak's arm moved lightly about her waist as he grinned at the younger man. 'You take it correctly, Rik.'

'That's great!' Rik bent to kiss Tyler warmly on the cheek. 'He's been moping around like a bear with a sore head the last couple of days,' he confided to her with an affectionate glance at his brother. 'You're a lucky man, Zak,' he congratulated as the two men shook hands.

'Your turn next.' Zak waggled his eyebrows suggestively at Rik.

'I'm happy as I am,' Rik protested.

'Is he?' Tyler whispered to Zak as Rik moved away to talk to one of the other actors who'd starred in *Gunslinger*.

'I'll tell you about it later,' Zak promised.

And Tyler didn't doubt that from now on they would tell each other everything.

No more secrets. Ever.

Exactly as it should be!

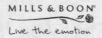

MILLS & BOON

Live the emotion

1105/01b

Modern
romance™

THE ITALIAN'S CONVENIENT WIFE
by Catherine Spencer

When Paolo Rainero's niece and nephew are orphaned he must protect them. A marriage of convenience to Caroline Leighton, their aunt, is his solution. But he must show Callie that he's changed since their fling nine years ago. Their mutual desire is rekindled – but Paolo feels that Caroline has a secret…

THE ANTONAKOS MARRIAGE *by Kate Walker*

An ageing tycoon is blackmailing Skye Marston into marriage – but she'll have one night of passion first… Theo Antonakos is furious when she slips away from him – and still furious when he goes to meet his stepmother-to-be. Only to find that they already know each other – in the most intimate way…

MISTRESS TO A RICH MAN *by Kathryn Ross*

Celebrity agent Marc Clayton knows a gold-digger when he sees one. And when gorgeous Libby Sheridan shows up, to cause a scandal for his top client, he knows he needs to keep her close – very close… Libby won't be bought off – but as their power struggle turns to passion Marc takes her out of the limelight…and into his bed!

TAMED BY HER HUSBAND *by Elizabeth Power*

Everyone thinks they know Shannon Bouvier – heiress, wild child, scandalous man-eater. And she's happy to let the world believe the lies. Kane Falconer thinks he knows her too. It's his job to tame Shannon – and this ruthless millionaire knows just how…

On sale 2nd December 2005
Available at most branches of WHSmith, Tesco, ASDA, Borders, Eason, Sainsbury's and most bookshops

Visit www.millsandboon.co.uk

FREE

4 BOOKS AND A SURPRISE GIFT!

We would like to take this opportunity to thank you for reading this Mills & Boon® book by offering you the chance to take FOUR more specially selected titles from the Modern Romance™ series absolutely FREE! We're also making this offer to introduce you to the benefits of the Reader Service™—

> ★ **FREE home delivery**
> ★ **FREE gifts and competitions**
> ★ **FREE monthly Newsletter**
> ★ **Books available before they're in the shops**
> ★ **Exclusive Reader Service offers**

Accepting these FREE books and gift places you under no obligation to buy; you may cancel at any time, even after receiving your free shipment. Simply complete your details below and return the entire page to the address below. You don't even need a stamp!

YES! Please send me 4 free Modern Romance books and a surprise gift. I understand that unless you hear from me, I will receive 6 superb new titles every month for just £2.75 each, postage and packing free. I am under no obligation to purchase any books and may cancel my subscription at any time. The free books and gift will be mine to keep in any case.

P5ZEE

Ms/Mrs/Miss/Mr..............................Initials ....
                                                    BLOCK CAPITALS PLEASE

Surname ....

Address ....

....

....Postcode ....

Send this whole page to:
The Reader Service, FREEPOST CN81, Croydon, CR9 3WZ